Springtime in

Autumn

3833-CHUC

Springtime in Autumn

John Chuchman

Contents

Poetry 11
Age and Time 12
Ascension 16
Awareness 18
Battle 22
Silence 24
Box 28
The Bridge 30
Brilliant Woman 34
Busyness 36
Metamorphosis 40
Caught? 42
Centrifugal Force 44
Challenge 45
Chaos 47
Circle of Welcome and Respect 49
Circles 51
Climb Down 52
The Climb 54
Conformity 57
Connection 59
Connections 61
Conventional Religion 63
A Cross to Bear 65
The Dance 67

Death and Life 69
With Dignity 71
Dilemma 73
Diversions 75
Drink 77
Emmaus—Their Grief 81
Emmaus—His Caregiving 83
Essence 85
The experience 86
Failure 88
Faith 89
False Self 90
The fire 92
Paths 94
The Four (Enneagram) that is Me. 96
Freedom 99
Full Life 100
Future Happiness 102
God is Love is God 104
God is One 107
God's Flashlight 108
Worrying about Children and Grandchildren 110
Challenge 111
Heart 113
Hell 115
Now 116
I am. 118
The difference 120
What's important? 123
Intuition 125
Savages? 126
Jesus Christ and Forgiveness 130
Path 134
Justice and Mercy 136
Role of the Laity 138

Reflection 140
Spiritual Leadership 142
Lord's Prayer 144
Love is 145
A Loving Connection 147
Merely Survive or Grow? 149
My Circular Mantra 150
Me 151
Moment 153
Mind 155
Moving Out to Get In 157
My Call to Awareness 159
Present Moment 161
Myths 164
Napoleon on St. Helena 165
Need 169
Oh, No 171
Old Man Winter 173
Open Table 175
Order 177
Paradox 179
An ever-changing past 181
Path 183
Paths 184
Paul 186
Pendulum 188
Pentecost 189
Pentecost 2 192
Picture Window 194
Plan 195
The Power 197
Stop Pretending 199
Puzzle 201
Quest 202
Questions 204

Reflection 205
Risk 207
Sacramental Moment 208
Sadness 211
Sailing through Life 213
Self 219
Shadows 221
Silence 223
Someone 225
Spark 226
Wind on the Water 227
Stand and Stare 228
Story 230
Stray 232
The Stream 235
The Sun 238
Who's terms? 239
Thirst 240
Together 242
My Friend, the Tree 243
Trust 245
Unquenchable? 246
Value 248
Viking Way 250
Whirlpool 252
Who? 253
Wholeness 254
Winds 256
Prayer 257
Wonder 258
Communicate 260
Poem 262

Springtime in Autumn is dedicated to all the people
who knowingly or unknowingly helped me in my spiritual
quest for true self and the Divine within.

Poetry

Poetry allows me to

find myself and
lose myself
at the same time.

In my poetry,
I discover a spiritual vitality that

lifts me above myself,
takes me out of myself,
makes me present to myself

on a level of being
I did not know I could ever achieve.

Would that it could do
the same for you.

Age and Time

Time!
Our obsession.
We spend it, waste it, invest it,
lose it and save it.
We worship time.
Yesterday is of little value;
Tomorrow looks priceless.
Some fail to live till they die;
Some died long before they were buried.

Our preoccupation with time
erodes our consciousness of the present moment.
Does life run out as time runs out or
Is life just starting—now?
There is no place to hurry to now but here,
And here and now is beautiful.

We live with new intensity,
not less.
We make every moment count.
We enjoy today.
We are fully present where we are.
Creation goes on creating;
And is valuable
in all dimensions, at all times, everywhere.

Busyness anaesthetizes us.
We become routinized and robotized.
Our spirituality calls us
To Consciousness,
To Awareness,
To Reflection,
Reflection on the meaning of the moment.

Age modulates life.
Reflection replaces engorgement.
Slowness becomes a virtue.
We learn to live again.
Slowing down is the beginning of life.
We see old things newly.
We come to peace with what we've done in life.
We know we've learned from
all we've done.
We Rejoice and Repent.
We Divest.
We get closer to center of self.
We contemplate what we have become and
What we have done
for others.
We Divest and become
Leaner and Truer.
We can do important things now,
not done yet because we were too important.
We now give ourselves to the world
We now do what needs to be done
only because it needs to be done.

We transcend.
Our individualism has been admirable,
But disenchanting.
In it, we worship ourselves.

Our individualism dims our consciousness of
the needs of others.
We even lose sight of the gifts of others,
by focusing on our own.
Now, we recognize and accept
our own weakness.
We discover dependence;
In it is the Glory of God and
The Whole human race.
Now we are learners,
generous givers,
caregivers,
lovers of life.
We transcend self and
Enter into the mystical meaning of
The Oneness of all life.

Eternity begins to feel like home as
We focus on the life to come.
By focusing on the life to come,
we slow down enough
to savor this one.
Now, wisdom supersedes knowledge
and
Life supersedes living.

Age is full of excitement and
Danger.
Some crumble and quit.
Some cease to be vital.
Some crawl down inside themselves and wait to die,
full of anger, despair, regret.
Instead,
We strive to the top of the mountain,
look down at the plains below and

Laugh.
There is no more climbing to do.
There is only the glory of the view.
We discover that
What we were searching for our whole life
Is deep within us.

Ascension

Baptism in the Spirit,
essential to our salvation
comes about at
Pentecost.

Jesus teaches
that he is the only one who can mediate the Spirit
since no one had ever
gone up into heaven.
The Holy Sprit comes about
only as a result of
Jesus being lifted up.

Jesus says that
only His return to the Father
will reveal His true origins
that God is the One who sent Him.

"Lifted Up"
conjures the crucifixion scene
where Jesus is lifted up from the earth
on the cross.
In John's Gospel,
"Lifted Up"
refers to one continuous ascent–

crucifixion, resurrection, ascension.
Jesus' Ascension:
Jesus lifted up on the cross
Jesus raised from the dead
Jesus lifted up into heaven.

Jesus ascension into heaven seen as vital by Him,
"It is much better for you if I go."
"If I fail to go, the Paraclete will never come to you,
whereas if I go,
I will send Him to you."

Only when Jesus is lifted up in Glory
would the communication of the Spirit
constitute a continuing source of life
for those who put their faith in Him.
"Eternal Life is given only
to those begotten from above—
life begotten of water and the *Spirit*."

Awareness

Anthony DeMello defined Spirituality as

Awareness.

The answer given his persistent questioning followers was
"Awareness, awareness, awareness."

How does it apply to me?

Do I inhabit the ultimate community of
inter-connected being called consciousness?
If I do,
I am aware or awareness.

How did I get here?

In infancy, I experienced little self-consciousness,
no real reflection.
As I grew, I became more "aware"
of myself.
But my awareness was dominated by
parents and family
and then into adolescence by my peers.

As a young adult,
I grew in self awareness, but
tended to be the center of my existence.

Adulthood brought awareness
of others.
My awareness of and even concern for others
was confined to family and friends and
I practiced selective compassion
on occasion.
I was still half–or more–asleep.
My knowledge, compassion, and love
still centered around me.

Late in life,
I occasionally was able to tap into
the state of consciousness where
creativity resides.
(That state is said to be the source of all inspiration,
poetry, art, music, literature, science, ad philosophy.)
Although, I could only sneak into that state of consciousness
occasionally and briefly,
it's power is awesome.

An exciting and sometimes scary aspect of this time of life for me
is a new willingness to go with intuition.
(My mind ignored or overruled or closed off my intuition
most of my previous life.)
I have told many that
I now believe the Holy Spirit speaks to us through intuition.
And then I read Wayne Teasdale's
"Intuition is itself the faculty of integration with
Infinite Consciousness."
Wow!

Are metaphysical awareness and intellectual illumination
intuitive forms of knowing?

Sometimes, my expanded awareness simply provides me
a greater knowledge of the mysteries surrounding my
existence.

Less frequently but more powerfully
my heart is even transformed by such awareness;
My heart and mind become integrated.
Wisdom, Love, Compassion join in
animating my consciousness.
My self-interest gives way to Love
through surrender.

Sometimes
The profound connections
made with the bereaved
seem to be connections with all of humanity
and even with God.
In compassion,
the moment seems to embrace all beings.

It seems the fullness of awareness.
It seems true
Spirituality.

Battle

My mind and heart do battle.

My mind analyzes my brokeness;
My heart makes me whole.

My mind tells me to shrink back;
My heart allows me trample the dragons.

My mind says the six directions allow me no way out;
My heart has traveled out thousands of times.

My mind haggles;
my heart sees thousands of markets beyond.

My heart reels from bliss to bliss;
my mind burns with dark denial.

My mind says, do not go forward,
annihilation contains only thorns;
my heart laughs because the thorns are only in my mind.

Silence, says my heart,
Enough words.

As I pull the thorn of existence out of my heart,

I see thousands of rose gardens,

in me.

Silence

All things begin in Silence.
All things end in Silence.
Silence takes me
to the core of life.

All true gifts
are given and received
in Silence.

Silence underlies, permeates all things
because
the Divine is Silent.

My poetry is like the moon
reflecting the light from
the Sun of Silence
to illumine hearts
beyond
concepts, dogmas, and words.

My poetry hopes to lead to
a point at which
one is prepared to jump into
the ocean of silence,
to a presence

which has no words.
My words are meant
to dissolve words,
to dissolve the need for
images.

I pray
Silence dances its fullest
in my poems.

My prayer is that
the reader of my poetry
1. Enters into the Divine Silence from which
my poems–and all things–come
2. Listens to the Divine within self
3. Moves to the deepest place
where the Divine Presence is always.

Sacred Art
is sacred
because it springs from
the most devoted Silence of Adoration,
moving through a Silence of Adoration,
leading to a Silence of Adoration.

Silence longs for action,
a fundamental iconoclasm
leading to Divine consciousness.

Silence longs not for
prayer or fasting,
something beyond rites and rituals,
beyond dogmas and concepts.
Silence longs for
inward meaning that transforms whole being

entering into the fire of inward meaning.
Sacred Art, thus,
demands action from within,
a return to
the Divine Silence
from which the Art came.
It demands
a profound act of receptivity.

My poetry craves
to point to
what can never be said in words,
what can never be held conceptually:
entry into Silence.

I strive to destroy the barriers
between words and hearts,
between silence and dogma.
Words do not say
what one thinks they say.

I wish listeners of my poetry to
leap to another dimension
to hear
the One talking
within.

Keep Silent;
The world of Silence is a vast fullness.
Do not beat the drum of words,
the empty drum.

Even the most glorious language,
the most glorious concepts,
the most glorious secrets

dissolve in the Silence
of
Divine Presence.
Like small candles,
they fade away
when the Great Sun comes up.

No more words!
Hear only the voice within.

I strive to create
an external space of words
which leads to
the only space that exists,
the space inside.

Every vision born of earth is fleeting.
Every vision born of heaven
is a Blessing.

Fill me with the wine of your Silence.
Let it soak my every pore.
The inner splendor it reveals
is a Blessing,
is a Blessing,
is a Blessing.

Don't move.
Stop the mind.
Enjoy the Blessing.

Box

I lived
in the Box
I built around myself,
feeling secure there.

Trouble is
I never grew beyond the box,
and worse,
staying in the box,
drew me apart
from love.

Holy Spirit
called me outside the box
(scary)
where I could grow
and
Love
and
be Loved.

I was tempted to stay in the box,
even shrink it
around me,
but

I knew I'd never grow.
I'd feel secure there,
and I suspect lonely,
and
I'd never see from the box
the horizons
that I quest.

Should have never built the box,
but maybe we all start out that way
and only grow
when we answer that call
to live our dreams
outside the box.

The Bridge

On this side, it is cold and dark.
I stood here with others
in the cold and darkness,
doubled over in pain.
Some developed an eating disorder
to cope.
I drank;
Some used drugs.
Some lost control of sexual behavior
to distract them from the pain.
Most of us developed an addiction
to power, to success, to control,
and focused on other addictive people.
I did not know about the bridge.
I thought I was trapped here.

> Then, by the Grace of God,
> my eyes were opened
> because it was time.

I saw the bridge.

> People told me
> what was on this side:
> warmth, light, and

healing from pain.

I could barely glimpse or imagine this,
but I decided to start the Quest
across the bridge.
I tried to convince those close to me
that there was a bridge to a better place,
but they wouldn't listen.
They couldn't see.
They would not believe.
They were not ready
for the Quest.

Despite years together,
I decided to go it alone
because I did believe
and
because people on this side
kept cheering me on.

The closer I got
to the other side,
the more I could see and feel that
what I had been promised
was real.

There was light, warmth,
and healing;
this was a better place.

Now there is bridge
between me
and
those on the other side.

Sometimes, I am tempted
to go back and
drag loved-ones over the bridge,
but it cannot be done.
No one can be dragged
across the bridge.

Each person must cross
at his or her own choice,
when the time is right,
if ever.
Some will come.
Some will stay here.
The choice is not mine.

I can love them;
I can wave to them;
We can holler back and forth.
I can cheer them on.

But I cannot make them
come over with me.

Standing in the light and warmth,
I do not have to feel guilty.
This is where I am meant to be.

I do not have to return to the darkness and pain
just because another's time
has not yet come.

The best thing I can do
is stay in the light because
it reassures others
that this is a better place

full of light and warmth and healing.

And
if others decide to cross the bridge,
I will be there to cheer them on.

In the meantime,
I pray for them and
We can at least meet
on the bridge.

3833-CHUC

Brilliant Woman

Always thought a brilliant woman
would be exciting!

The stereotypical
passive subservient acquiescent female
may be full of love,
but also unfulfilled.

The brilliant woman I know
lights up the world around us
and
provides powerful insights
to life's challenges.

Trouble is
her truly penetrating questions
are not easily answerable
and
she refuses to accept the easy answers anyway.

My attempts to answer her insightful
persistent questions
force me to a depth within me
very dark
and rarely, if ever, explored.

And
not every thing there is pleasant.

Thus,
my brilliant female friend,
Wisdom,
is truly a soulmate
taking us both
on a journey deep within
where
our true selves reside.

I must be willing
to bring up from my depths
all that is there
exposing it to the light
of her brilliance.

Courage, John, courage!

Busyness

When I am busy,
I feel "in charge,"
I believe I am important,
I become indispensable and necessary,
My ego is assured that I am productive,
that I am accomplishing something worthwhile and valuable.

By being efficiently busy helping others,
I can accept even more tasks,
help even more people,
I can escalate the demands on my time, attention, care.

When I project a state of busyness,
Others notice how important or helpful I am and
Either do not disturb me or
Seek me out for something even more important.

I just love being busy.

Trouble is,
When I am in a state of busyness,
I tend not to really notice my surroundings or
Other people,
I tend to be unresponsive to
the *True* needs of those who cross my path,

Or even
My Own True Needs.

When I am in a state of busyness,
I lose my contemplative attitude and
deprive myself of
Moments of Beauty, Surprise, Delight, and Love.

When I am busy being busy,
I avoid making time for
Leisure, Play, Relationships or Reflection.
I take delight in moving fast,
being caught up in a rhythm that
overwhelms my internal sense of self and
my felt response to
internal and external events.

In busyness,
I am actually captivated by a consciousness
largely generated by a culture outside me,
a *false* consciousness.
If I can avoid busyness and
experience a Contemplative attitude,
A Creative Leisure,
Recollection,
Mindfulness,
I can become *Centered,*
Relaxed, Serenely Present and Mindful,
I am able to Delight in the day
as it unfolds,
I am able to receive each person who enters my space
with *Loving Mercy.*

I inhabit an Enlarged Contemplative Awareness.
When I move out of busyness,

God is present to me in the world
As in my heart.

But,
To see God there–in the world–requires
My *Profound Attentiveness*;
I need a quality of heart that
enables me to see
the *invisible* and
A quality of presence in the precious present
that is *Aware* of
All that is *really* there.

Oh my,
In busyness,
I do not participate in the deep dimensions
of my experiences.

How to I escape this trap
of busyness?

To grow,
I must.

Metamorphosis

Does the caterpillar
resist becoming a butterfly
for fear of change
or
fear of falling?

Or does it show faith
by becoming what it is meant to become
and risk the change.

There is security in the cocoon.
Who knows what dangers lurk out there?

Having been forced to crawl on the ground,
it knows it cannot fly,
yet in being willing to be transformed,
to let go of what was,
it grows into a
beautiful new creature of God,
capable of doing things
it never dreamed possible.

It had to die to its old self
to be born anew.
It had to be willing to let go of what was

so that what could be
is.

Fear change,
fear falling,
and
never fly.

Be willing to change,
to be free,
and to grow
into a new and beautiful creation of God,
what you are meant to be.

Caught?

Having taken numerous detours,
having made many missteps,
having wasted precious living waters,
having run towards mirages,
but now thirsting even more,
willing to accept the unknown,
even move to it, through it,
willing to follow this path wherever, however,
my heart runs faster than my feet.

I say I am the sum total of my past experiences.
Am I?
But if I am, do they trap me?

Oh, that no moments were related.
That succession did not exist.
That effect does not follow cause.
That each moment is separate,
independent, unique, unrelated
to any other in the universe
of time and space.

Otherwise,
the past tends to trap.
My feet stick in its muck.

It's clinging vines grab at my ankles and
keep me from following my heart.
All the causes in my past
lead to effects now and in the future.
Or do they?

If the past does not exist
and if the future does not exist
and I am forever trapped in this present moment,
How can the past bind me?
Or is it me that binds me
from the past, to the past?

The muck the slows me,
the vines that grab my ankles,
all the things I did in that time that no longer exists,
may exist only in my mind.

I may be as free to move up
as I ever was.

Guess what, I am.

Centrifugal Force

The faster I go,
the more outward I am thrown
Away from center.

Only when I slow
do I move towards my center
To God within me.

Challenge

In my search for my identity,
I tended to make my projects
absolute.
I tended to see others
as stepping stones
to achieve my projects.
In essence, I made my projects
ultimate;
I idolize them.

All around me in creation is God's challenge
to grow.
God's call to growth
comes through all those around me.
By opening up
to God's others
I dis-idolize my own project,
make it relative,
die to myself a bit and
grow.

I never know where opening up to others will lead;
I tend to want to rest on any new plateau,
to make my new project
absolute and ultimate,

but there always is more other,
more gift,
more challenge
to keep growing.

Dying to myself or my project
is painful.
Stretching to meet the needs of others
is not easy.
Yet, the challenge is always there.

In the battle between idolatry, self, project,
and suffering.
Christ sided with suffering.
Guess He showed the way.

Chaos

When will I learn
that feeling unsettled
is good;
that restlessness
connotes thirst
for God;
that
Life is a Quest is a Quest is a . . ?

How do I get rid of this desire
to be comfortable;
to have things settled and in order;
to know what's happening
and why?

Things are never settled very long anyway,
if at all;
and maybe only in my mind.
So why am I trying to get the cosmos
to conform to my idea
of peace?

Even the sun as center of this solar system
is not at peace,
not at rest,

not settled.
And I am not the center of the universe anyway.

Somehow
God orders the chaos or
the chaos follows God's order or
God keeps the chaos under control or . .
Whatever.

The peace I seek can only be found in the Center,
In God.
So enjoy being unsettled.
It IS what's happening and
God's in control.

That is true Faith,
isn't it?

Or is it?

Circle of Welcome and Respect

Let's form a circle and join hands.

Feel our connection with the Universe!

We are conscious self-reflective beings
of the Universe.

We belong here; we are not mistakes.

We are the products of
15 billion years of evolution.

Feel the connection with Mother Earth.

This is our home planet.

We have a right to take our place
with–not over–
all other beings and
one another.

We have a right to be
loved, cherished, and respected.

Look at each other.

See the diversity.
We are all different.

The most observable fact about the world
is its respect and love of diversity.

Feel loved here.
You are cherished here.
You are respected here.
You are safe here.

Circles

Circles, circles everywhere
Different sizes, yet each complete.

Why do we keep trying with
Lines and squares and pyramids
to make our way?

God, a Circle of Love,
Surrounds us.
We cannot box God in;
We cannot find God at the top of some pyramid;
We cannot draw a line separating anyone from God's Love.

See the circles;
Learn the circles;
Live a circle . . .
Of Love.

Climb Down

I know He is around.
I can feel His presence.
Others must also;
crowds are gathering.

No way can I approach Him;
My life has been a litany of faults, failures, sins.
Maybe, just a look, a glance.

I need to see Him.
I must.

I think I can climb that tree and
rise above the tumult.

It's a struggle to get high enough,
but if I do, I may be able to see Him.

Ah,
It's more peaceful up here, quieter.
There's less of a hassle above the crowd.

There!
I see Him!
I can see Him!

He sees me, too.
He looks at me and says,
"John come down from on high."
"Descend, for this day I am with you in your house."

Wow!
I thought I had to rise up above all the others to see Him,
and he tells me to
descend.
He tells me to be with Him
in my own house!

I come down quickly,
retreating to my own place
where, indeed,

He is with me.

The Climb

Climbing up
The Mountain of Life,
each of our paths is unique.

And each path takes many turns,
sometimes sideways,
sometimes even down
before heading up again.

Each path is fraught with hazards
and stumbling blocks.
Often I trip,
am stymied,
fall
and hang on for dear life.

I'm often tempted
to stop climbing
and build a little cabin or chateau or
even set up a tent
just to rest and enjoy the view.
But I know
I cannot stop.
I must keep climbing.

Trouble is
I cannot see what's on top.
The Cloud of the Unknowing
keeps me from seeing my goal.
It takes Faith
and
Love
and courage
to pierce it.

Along the way,
I encounter many others,
each on his/her own path.
Sometimes our paths run parallel
and we help each other
as we stumble.
Sometimes our paths cross
and we share experiences and
provide guidance.

We help light each other's path.

As I encounter
and help others
on the way,
there seems a tendency
to want to hang on to them,
to bring them on my path,
or even take their path with them.

Sometimes the love I feel
from encountered travelers
drives me to want to merge our paths.

But I know
this cannot be.

Each path is unique.

Leaving mine for another's path
or
forcing another on my path
is
but a detour
in life.

Learning how to let go
is
a critical lesson I am learning
in climbing
The Mountain of Life.

Leaving behind the security
found in an other
is tough.
But I know
it is a false security.
I know that I must take my own path
through the Cloud of the Unknowing
to my ultimate destination.

And I know,
although each path is unique,
all paths lead to the same place,
to Love,
to God.

I know that
Letting Go
allows each of us
to find our way
so we CAN all be together again.

Conformity

God's in heaven
and all's right with the world.
We get that feeling
when things are going our way.

If sun shines on our picnic,
God is good.
If our kids marry well,
life is good.
If we're healthy,
things are they should be.

My measure of how good is life
is its conformity
with my plans,
my desires,
my happiness.

Yet,
Does the oak tree bemoan the loss of the acorn?
Does the butterfly rue the death of the caterpillar?
Are lions and tigers to blame for feeding on their prey?
Do organ donors resent the loss of their given body parts?
Does the young adult wish for the teenage years?
Rebirth requires death, death to the old.

To deny death is to not fully live life.

God does not make bad things happen to good people.
God sees to it that from each "bad" thing that happens.
some good results.

It may be that there are no "good" or "bad" events in life,
that they are two sides of the same event.

Giving up the preoccupation with
having things go my way,
I can be free to ride the wind,
to ride the waves,
to be happy with things as they are.

In any case,
none of the events which seem so tragic
or so glorious or joyful
are very important
in the overall scheme of things.
They are microscopic dots
in the universe.

So why get upset?
The creator is in control, not I.
And do I really think He'll reorder the Universe
to suit me?

Connection

Every time I have contact with an other,
it seems to me that the connection
either enhances that person's self esteem
or
diminishes it.

Seems like one or the other happens
with no in-between.

It also seems to me that
with each contact
I make with an other,
I also either
grow
or
diminish.

The important revelation for me is that
I cannot grow
while diminishing an other,
nor
can I be diminished
by
enhancing an other.

This discovery
has brought new light to
any and all connections I make.

Connections

I have come to the realization
through experience
that
what is the most personal,
what is the deepest in us,
what seems to be the most private
is in fact
the most universal.

And when we share
that which is the deepest and most personal in us
in love,
we truly connect with one another,

and not just with one another,
but with all of humanity,

and probably, with
God.

Conventional Religion

has trained us
to rely on external authority,
which often does nothing for God
or
our own spiritual growth.

The promise of the Holy Spirit
is the promise of
Inner Authority.

Many good people are taught
that to trust or believe in God
means
to believe or trust in things
external to oneself.

In the Catholic tradition,
people have been taught
to put their trust in the hierarchy
forgetting that *they* are church.
Protestants look to the bible.
Both church and bible are fonts of truth
and ought to be profoundly respected, but
they are a step removed from
the inner testimony of the Holy Spirit.

We cannot avoid that responsibility.

Some people use external authority as an excuse
not to walk the inner journey and
discover their true souls.
(Some in church hierarchy foster external reliance
for obvious reasons.)

The church is filled with people living on hearsay,
on someone else's authority,
not knowing what they themselves know.

We must go within
to connect to the Divine in us,
to discover God's Love and
the Wisdom of the Holy Spirit.

A Cross to Bear

Carrying my cross
does not mean
humbly resigning myself to
pain, misery, and sorrow.

It does not mean
accepting life's trials and tribulations,
its challenges and its setbacks
as givens.

It does not mean
wearing my sorrow, sickness, sadness
in order to elicit
sympathy, commiseration and pity.

To me,
Carrying my cross means
expressing the fullness of my faith
despite the chides, mocking, derision, scorn, jeering,
ridiculing, sneering, belittling, and abuse
of others.

To me, it means
being proud enough to stand up for my faith,
being enthusiastic enough to share it,

being confident enough to express it.
To me, Carrying my Cross means
not accepting the bad things that happen,
but rising above them and
seeing the good that flows from them
(thanks to God.)

I hold up the Cross,
not as a symbol of suffering and death,
but as a symbol of a resurrected and living Faith,
a symbol of Joy!

The Dance

If I can only let go
of my obsession
in trying to think what it all means,
I might be able to hear the music
and join in the dance.

I don't have to go far
to hear the music.
When I am alone on a starlit night,
When I see migrating birds,
When I see roses bloom,
When I see my granddaughters
being children, really children,
When I see Torch Lake,
calm as a mirror reflecting the cosmos
or wild as the ocean,
When I know Love–
At such moments,
An awakening,
A turning aside of judgements,
Newness, Emptiness, Purity of Vision
provide the music
and a glimpse of the dance.

The more I persist in misunderstanding life,
the more I try to analyze things into strange finalities
with complex purposes of my own,
the more I involve myself
in sadness, absurdity and despair.

But,
it doesn't matter
because no analysis of mine can change the reality of things
or stain the joy of the dance
which is always there.

Indeed,
I am in the midst of it
and
It is in the midst of me;
It beats in my very blood
whether I want it to or not.

I have been invited
to forget myself,
cast my awful analyses and explanations to the winds
and
enjoy the dance.

Join me?

Death and Life

It is possible to suffer with dignity
or without.

Many do not understand
The Art of Suffering
and instead
experience a thousand fears,
ceasing to be alive,
filled with fear, bitterness, hatred, and despair.

We must
Come to Terms with Life.
Death must be seen
as a part of life.

Life can be extended by death.
By accepting death as a part of life,
We no longer waste energies on
fear of death or
a refusal to accept its inevitability.

By excluding death from life,
We cannot live a full life.
By admitting death into our life,
We enlarge and enrich it.

An acceptance of what must come
affords us the opportunity
to live now fully
and
to appreciate it thoroughly.

With Dignity

Let me go
with Dignity.

Unless you connect me
with my Mother,
Don't connect me to
anything.
Do not connect me to
a heartless machine;
That's undignified.

Let me go with pride
with joy,
with a sense of fulfillment,
and most important of all,
with dignity as
a Loving Human Being.

Connect me up to
a glorious computer
and you preserve,
not me,
but the machine,
and in the process,
allow it to siphon and suck and drain

what is supposed to be me.
The cord originally was cut
with Love;
Don't attempt to re-attach it
in fear.

Dilemma

Having spent most of my life
safe within the boundaries,

the Holy Spirit now seems to call me
to seek horizons.
A scary adventure,
which tests my Faith.
Exciting!

Then,
I meet one
who has been hurt much in life
who seeks asylum and safety
within the boundaries.

We cannot really connect
because
the boundaries of his security–
such as it is–
become barriers
to me.

Frustration!

How can I help if he won't let me in?
How can I love him
if he will not venture out of the box?

I cannot abandon my quest for the horizons,
cannot force myself into his cocoon, and
cannot pull him out into the open.

Tell me what to do.
Please.

Diversions

Every time
I get excited about
moving in a certain direction,
about pursuing a selected path,
about devoting time and effort
to a desired project,
God
seems to laugh.

Sometimes God lets me run the gamut
sometimes not.
Often,
as I'm rushing headlong
in a direction I'm sure is right,
God simply
calls from a new direction,
calls me to a new path,
diverts me
in a way I'd not imagined.

When will I learn?
When will I let go
of my way?
When will I simply accept
the guidance

that is all around me?
When will I learn
to have enthusiasm,
not for an arrival,
but for the journey.
And that the journey
is
not a straight line,
but one with many paths,
up, down, forward, back,
round and round?

When will I learn
not to try and see God
in an arrival,
but to see God,
in my journey?

Drink

Alone on a mountain
in Black Canyon City
seeking an answer.

The question came from nowhere,
or did it?
Isn't it time to stop drinking?
Why?

Oh, I supposed I could.
I had often stopped in the past,
for a month or so,
just to make sure I could.
God know's I'd had my share of alcohol through the years—
more than my share.
Why the call to stop now?

Alone up here in the high desert,
it's cold at night.
I hiked during the day,
was tired,
and so snuggled under the covers
as the sun set
and fell asleep.
Was it the wind howling outside that woke me up?

Eleven PM by the clock.
"Come to the chapel, John."
What?!
You've got to be kidding, I thought.
That would require getting dressed
and trekking through the night cold
to get to the stand-alone chapel.
It could wait till tomorrow, I thought.

Nope!
Sleep was not to come.

Got dressed,
Opened the door to what seemed like
a snow-covered landscape.
The snow moved not at all in the blowing wind,
as it was simply the brilliant reflection of
a marvelous full moon.

To the chapel,
unlock the door,
remove my jacket,
kneel and pray.

I could stop drinking whiskey,
limiting my intake to beer and wine.
Or
I could drink only at restaurants or at friend's,
not drinking at home.
Nope,
Never have been a half-way kind of guy.
Either I stop or I don't?

But why?
Didn't get an answer,

or did I?
What I got was,
"If you want to heal, be healed."
What?

Oh, if I really expected to help others,
I needed to be free myself,
free from any addictions.
Oh!

That simple?

I did want to help others.
And although I was not an alcoholic
(at least I did not think I was)
I handled alcohol less well as I grew older
and
I often did not know when to stop.
So why not?

Ok, God,
if that's what you want,
I'll do it.
But it may very difficult after all these years,
so I'll need your help.

Got up,
started to put my jacket on,
"John, come back and pray some more."
OK
Knelt a while longer and
confirmed by decision.

Seemed OK to leave now.
Leaving the chapel,

I locked the door,
turned around into the now still night air
to make my way across the moonlit path
back to my hermitage,

When there among the millions and millions
of stars in the black desert sky
shooting across my path was
the brightest, the most beautiful
shooting star
I had ever seen.

Shivers!
Goose bumps!
Chills!

Oh Wow!

The decision was right;
The decision was blessed.
Amen.

November 8, 1992
Haven't had a drink since.
Thanks, God.

In order to heal,
be healed.
And
Heal and be healed.

Emmaus

Their Grief

The minds and hearts of the disciples
on their way to Emmaus
were filled with distress.

Their Master had been crucified.
Their hope for the future had been killed.

He had called them; they answered His call.
They followed Him in Love with hope.

Jesus' death was failure.
Their dreams for the future were dashed.

And they had deserted Him.
They had run away when He needed them.

They felt guilt.
They felt shame.
They let their friend and master down.

They were leaving Jerusalem
to escape their pain.

They suffered disappointment.
They suffered guilt and shame.
Their future was lost.

They grieved.

Emmaus

His Caregiving

The Easter journey for them was now to begin.

The Risen Lord met them where they were.
He met them at the heart of their depression.
He met them at the heart of their passion and pain.

This is the meaning of Caregiving:
To be with the Bereaved
wherever they may be;
To wait with them
whatever distress, pain, and guilt
assail them;
To be with them as Companion.

As with the Risen Lord,
Caregivers must be with the bereaved
as Companion, not as judge, not as spectator.

The Risen Christ did not try to "teach" the disciples,
nor give them a lesson.

He invited them to express their feelings;

thus He could enter their minds and hearts and
Suffer their passion with them.

It was not important that they recognize the Lord,
but that they could share their distress.

He let them be themselves.
He welcomed and accepted them.
A true Companion!

Essence

The essence of God
is peace beyond all knowing,
silence beyond all imagining,
depth of Love and security beyond description.

This essence
is always present,
and
knowing it
brings the most profound tranquility.

The nature of God
is extravagant generosity
of the most outrageous kind;
Millions of worlds and dimensions
out of divine joy.

Totally generous Love
is God.

The experience

The experience of Love
changed everything.

It seems to have come out of nowhere,
unexpectedly and undeservedly.
Unearned, it came.

And as it did,
it changed every thing, everything.

The formerly important things
simply slipped into
insignificance.

My awareness has been heightened;
Color came to my cheeks;
My heart beats faster–even skips a few now and then.
Thoughts, ideas, visions, dreams, fantasies
of my beloved
fill me all the day–and all the night.

This is love is an ocean;
I am but a minnow
in it.

It permeates all of me,
all of my body,
my being,
my spirit,
my essence.
It defines me.

Is it a flash of lightning
that I'm trying to hang on to?
Is it a rose
whose fragrance I want to retain beyond its life?
Is it a momentary glimpse of the vision of God
or Is it life-changing?
Or all of the above?

I don't know,
but I do know that
just as I cannot explain it or define it,
I cannot, must not, question it,
nor
challenge it.
I am to live in this love.
I am.
I am.

Failure

One of the greatest obstacles
to my growth
has been the fear of
making a fool of myself.

I now risk failure
hoping to grow to a point where
I might be able to risk
total failure.

Faith

Not a set of dogmas
Not a set of beliefs
Not something cast in concrete never changing
Not a code of conduct
Not a set of rituals
Not a credo
Not the port in a storm.

Faith is

Sailing the rough seas
Trusting in God
Being comfortable in uncertainty
Willingness to Change
Awareness of the Guidance around us
Acceptance of what is
Letting go
Acting on Intuition
Loving Unconditionally.

False Self

Am I really making the trip
from hypocrisy to sincerity,
from self-deception and ignorance and illusion
to self-honesty, clarity, and truth?

Or am I simply deceiving myself?

What really motivates me? Why?
My false self?

In my ministry,
Am I simply seeking
security, affection, esteem, power, control, and
a sense of self-worth?

How much I am conditioned by my ego!

Some say
I do not have to conquer my false-self.
Whew!
They say I simply have to observe it.
They say in observing it and being aware of it,
I can transcend its grip on me
and move toward my own transformation in
Love and Compassion.

Is that true?

I believe I am motivated by
Love and Compassion for others, but
Has my false-self distorted my sense of reality?

I am told we all have a shadow side,
but that the spiritually mature person
achieves a clear perspective on that shadow.
Have I?

Mother Teresa said,
"I realized I had a Hitler within me."
This was the basis of her transcendence.

My false self has hidden agendas,
programs for happiness.
I guess I need to keep these exposed;
I need to stay aware of these.

God, please keep me aware!

The fire

St. John of the Cross

compares our soul
to a log of wood,
dank, dirty, covered with moss.

The log cannot burn
before the darkness is smoked out of it.
At this point,
the flame is not bright to the soul, but dark.

It is not delectable to the soul, but acrid.

It brings neither refreshment nor peace,
but consumes and accuses it.

Neither is it glorious,
bu insidious and bitter.

This stage is difficult and full of grief,
but with the burning
wounding us to heal us.

Then the fire of Love
strips the log

and enters it.
A burning of Love and ecstasy then occurs.

The birth into Divine Life occurs.

Paths

Having overcome the temptation
to stop too long in a comfortable spot along the way
in a cabin or chateau
on my climb up life's mountain,
I am still faced with decisions
about which fork in the path
to take.

Makes no difference
I can rationalize to myself
as all paths lead to the same place,
the same ending.

Yet, if the journey is what it's all about
and not the arriving,
then the choice of which path to take is key.
And what if one of the forks
takes me back to the beginning?
(Do I believe in re-incarnation?)

I know where no fork leads;
And I know that as attractive as one fork may appear at the
onset,
it is does not presage the difficulty which may lie ahead.
And I know

from experience
that continuing on a path without challenge
often leads to
lack of growth
up the mountain.
(Circling because it's the easiest thing to do
doesn't make a lot of sense.)

So,
on what basis do I choose the fork to take?

My mind is of little value it seems
as what has happened to me before
offers little clue as to
what may come.

And what I see happening to others
may not apply to me.

I have felt the Holy Spirit
work in me through intuition.
I guess
I will just rely on intuition,
on the Holy Spirit
at work in me.

This must be what Faith is.

The Four (Enneagram) that is Me.

Melancholy
A tendency to mood swings
from depression to its denial and
an affected, high spirited excitement.

Extreme self-consciousness,
absorbed in my own limitations.

Thoughtful and reflective,
pensive and quietly reflective.

Sullen, irascible, ill-natured,
subtle touchiness.

Gracious friendliness,
cooperative spirit.

Romantic
Exaggeration of events, feelings, actions.
Enlarging events to heroic and adventurous proportions.

Over-dramatizing.

Drama: a view of life as a play
made up of a series of events that come together.

A Four

A sense of not measuring up, being incompetent.
Life is a series of efforts to make myself worthy.

A great fear:
anger and disruption in the environment.
I want that all human relationships blend into
an organic moving unity.
Anger, hate, misunderstanding, violence
hinder that flow.

The instinct to do.
Activity dominates.
A response to do remains instinctive.
Respond to life by doing something.

Although it is important to process experience,
reflecting and bending back on what has happened
in order to know what it was and how it affected me,
it falls away to activity.

Dance to the rhythmic motion of the universe
which can only be known when
the noise of compulsed activity grows silent.
Questions die away to
what is.

My self-worth grows around being able
to care for or organize or produce
in order to belong to the community of persons.

I feel special.
What happens to me seems unique and original.

The ordinary is frightening;
Intensity is the stuff of life for me.
Better a miserable day
than an ordinary one.

I look on and into events and
find succeeding moments, days, and years
laden with significance.
Nothing seems exempt from intensity.

All reality leads to growth or diminishment
and conscious of that,
I tend to over-dramatize events
in romance, anguish and crisis.

Freedom

When I began to understand that
I had nothing special to say,
I became free.

Speech and Silence became equally easy.

Whatever I can say
probably has been said before;
Whatever I can hear
probably has been heard before.

When I stop depending on being heard
or being thought of,
I realize that
I used to believe that speech and communication
gave me existence.

They do not.

Full Life

To live my life fully,
I now know
I must first go
into the mystical,
into the light,
into the transcendent consciousness
and then return
with the light,
fully conscious,
infusing the most ordinary details of my life
with sweetness and joy,
peace and ecstasy.

I now know
it is not enough
simply to shatter my false self.

What has to be done
is to unify the Light
with my ordinary daily life.
In doing so,
I share something of the completeness
in being of God.

God is immanent and transcendent,

in the world and beyond it,
acting and thinking in me–
and all others.
Yet, God is
entirely beyond the creation,
in the eternal glory
of the eternal light.

But so am I!
I am in this body
and transcendent.
The key is
to live at ease in all dimensions
and to let the transcendent dimension
flood through all my actions, thoughts, and feelings.

This is the full life.

Future Happiness

I spent much of my life
planning for,
anticipating,
working towards
happiness in my future.

Late in life–
but not too late–
I made the astonishing discovery that
there is no happiness in my future.

There is no happiness in any future.
Happiness can never be
somewhere else, sometime other.
Happiness can only be now,
in the precious present.

And
Searching for happiness
voided me of it.
By living in the future,
I avoided the happiness in the present.

I discovered that
In order to be Happy,

I must be present.
I must be present to myself
and present to others;
Present to myself Now
and
Present to others as Gift.

Despite my recollections of an event-filled past
and
My anticipation of a glorious future,
I found myself
Trapped,
Forever
in this uni-moment called Now
with no chance of escaping.

By letting my mind
take me elsewhere,
it robbed me
of the very thing I sought,
Happiness.

To be Happy,
I only need to stay put,
to be where and when I am,
to be Here and Now

God is Love is God

God must know how difficult it is for me
to love a God I cannot see or hear or touch.
So, God gives me others to love
and others who love me.

Trouble is,
God expects me to love all
and without condition,
as conditional love is not love at all.
Unconditional Love
is true Love,
is Divine.

In Loving,
I confirm I am a child of God,
as are all others.

In Loving,
I know God.

Any of my acts,
however righteous,
are fruitless without Love.
Loveless acts
are Godless acts.

God's Love is not a secret.
Jesus is sent
so that I and all others
may live eternally.

In my humanity,
I am not capable of True Love;
It is only of God.

Jesus atoning for my sins
is True Love.
I am to Love all others
in the same way Jesus Loves me.

No one sees God,
but when I Love an other (without condition),
I share Divine Love and
God lives in my heart.
When I Love an other,
God's Love, perfect in its giving,
is made perfect in its receiving.

The way I know God lives in my heart
and I Love and live in God,
is through the Holy Spirit.

I see,
I testify,
that Jesus is the Savior of the world.
When I acknowledge it,
not so much in word,
but in deed,
God lives in me
and
I in God.

I know,
I rely on
God's Love for me.

God is Love.
When I live in Love,
God lives in me
and
I in God.

God is One

The sun divides itself
through all the windows of my house.
If I draw the drapes,
multiplicity vanishes.

Multiplicity exists in the grapes,
not in the wine.

Alive in the light of God,
the death of my body
is grace.

My death is a wedding
with eternity.

God's Flashlight

Perhaps, I can be God's flashlight.

Maybe I can help light the way
for others
with the hand of God pointing me in the right direction.
I seem to help others,
not be instructing or directing,
but simply
by helping others see what's already there
in front of them
and all around them.

The energy source,
a touch of the Divine,
is within me.
I am switched on
by the hand of God.

I am rechargeable and
need periodic recharging.
I get recharged through other by getting plugged into
the ultimate energy source,
God's Love.

Maybe the light from within me

can help light the way for others
as it also helps me on my journey.

My light might also provide some warmth
as it opens a path through the darkness.

I am fulfilled only
as an instrument of help and guidance
and
I corrode and die with non-use.

Worrying about Children

and Grandchildren

I am not given a full understanding of life.
Only the courage to live it.

I have not been guaranteed the love of my children.
Only the strength to try and win and hold it.

With confidence
I know they will ultimately succeed,
that they will bear fruit in due season,
when the time is ripe.

For some of my children and grandchildren,
there will be second or third seasons,
(the more exotic the plant, the longer the wait)
But for all

it will be in God's time,

not mine.

Challenge

The big challenge I face
is making my life
an embodiment of
Wisdom, Compassion, Love.

The truths I have discovered
on my journey
need to find visible expression in my life.
Every one of my thoughts, words, actions
holds the possibility of being
a living expression of love.

I know it's not enough
to be a possessor of some wisdom.
Believing myself to be a custodian of some truth
makes me stale, self-righteous, rigid.

I have not been able to live in enlightened retirement
on the bounty of past achievements.

Wisdom is only alive
when it is lived.

Understanding is only liberating
when it is applied.

My portfolio of religious experiences is useless
unless it carries me through
loss, change, growth.

My knowledge and my achievements
matter little
unless
I touch the heart of an other
and
am touched by an other.

Heart

Closed to Love,
the heart stays small,
desiring little,
giving little,
growing not at all.

Love
expands the heart,
not only filling it,
but also increasing its capacity
to love and be loved.

In being Loved,
the Heart
expands beyond
the love experienced
so that
its need for love
is multiplied
and
its thirst for more
increased beyond imagination.

The thirst for more
seems unquenchable

but
survives
only by loving.

In Loving,
I am loved,
with that Love
increasing both
my ability to Love
and
my need for more.

Hell

Hell must be where
No one has anything in common with anyone else,
except that they hate each other
and
cannot get away from each other
and
themselves.

Now

The past is sweet
with many wonderful memories
and some not so sweet,
even painful.
But the past
is past . . .

It no longer exists.

If I dwell there,
either on the sweet or sorrowful,
I dwell in a time and place
that does not exist.

The future will be better.
I've worked hard to make it so.
I'm planning the future.
I look forward to it.
It will be good.

Or will it?

The future does not exist.

If I dwell there,

in all the possibilities,
all the *What If's,*
I dwell in a time and place
that does not exist.

When so many of my thoughts
take me to the past or future,
I have little or no time
to think of the present moment.

Yet, all that ever exists is
the precious present moment,
the Now.

If everything I will ever need
is available in the present moment,
here and Now,
I need to be here
Now.
This is where God is,
Here,
Now.

I am.

I'm not what I do
I'm told.

Big adjustment in thinking required
as it's easy to identify with
what I did–
the good stuff at least.

As if my activities
somehow justify me,
earn my way,
make up for
the things I didn't do–
or did badly.

Contrary to the programming,
We don't live a meritocracy.
Work hard, do good
guarantees nothing in life,
let alone the after-life.

So,
If I'm not what I do,
Who am I?

Some ask,
What one word defines me?

Has to be "Love,"
or at least related to "Love."
But "Lover"
doesn't sound right,
seems boastful and too one sided.
I need it as much–or maybe more—
than I crave giving it.

So then I'm told
to find a one-word modifier
to that defining word.

I thirst a thirst
I think will not be sated in this life.

Perhaps I'm just an

Insatiable Lover
(Questing Divine Love.)

Only God thirsts more . . .
. . . for me.
Whew.

The difference

How am I different than all of God's creation,
all of God's other creatures?

Other creatures use tools,
gather, communicate, care for the young,
are violent.

Is it my ability to *imagine* that distinguishes me?
Is it my *imagination* that places me a bit higher?

Am I unique in all of creation
because I can envision
what was, what might have been, what could be?

Some say
Imagining what might be can make it happen.

Trouble is we often imagine
great good or terrible evil
with reckless abandon,
without accountability.

Is imagination merely a step along the way
in my planning to do
or

does my imagining enable the outcome?
It is a gift.

But wait;
I thought Love was the greatest gift.
No other creature loves–
I think.

Love–true love, unconditional love–
must be unique to humankind.
It surely must be the greatest gift.

But are imagination and Love related,
intimately bound together?

True love transcends failings,
asks nothing in return,
is boundless.

No earthly object of my love
is without fault or failing.
What is that allows me to Love
despite imperfections in my beloved?

Imagination?

Does imagination allow me to see my beloved as perfect?
Or at least to allow me to believe that the faults and failings I
see
make no difference?
Is it imagination that allows me to believe
I might be loved unconditionally?
(It takes quite an imagination to see
someone loving me unconditionally
with all my faults and failings.)

But Love is of God.
God is Love.

Do I envision something of God
when I love an other unconditionally?
Maybe seeing something of God in an other is necessary
to love.
Seeing God in an other, surely takes
imagination.

And if imagination actually makes it happen,
if imagining God in an other actualizes Love,
then it truly is what makes us different
and
Imagination and love are intimately bound.

So,
Imaging God in my beloved,
actualizes my Love
of other
and
God.

What's important?

Why is it so important
to find True Self?

JFK, Jr. dies;
Friends lose a daughter
killed by a hit-and-run driver;
I look out at the stars of the universe and
feel insignificant.
My computer crashes and I feel detached.

My True Self is in others;
in knowing, loving, doing for others,
but
Why?

I yearn to be able to find a way to
Let my Granddaughters know my love,
to know Love.
I love my daughter, ache with her.

My friend the Tree
stands tall in the moonlight,
in the starlight left after the moon set
and
worries not about "why?" or about "significance,"

or about finding its True self.

It's not all about me
or
Is it?
If a touch of the Divine is within me—
and all others—
then, well,
Isn't it really all about me?

Oh, to give Glory to God
by just "being."

The mind is a curse.

"Just Love, John, Just Love."

Intuition

I am learning
to act in such a way that

Thought does not interfere
between me and what I do.

I now do
without thinking about it.
I try
to be in touch with
what the situation demands.
I just try and meet it.

I've had to get rid of
lots of useless thinking, reasoning, explaining, and
putting labels on things.

I am learning
to go with intuition.

Savages?

Creator of all things,
Ruler of all,
We ask you to listen to our words.
What you have made is returning to you.
It is rising to you
to show that our words are true.

Please listen to the words of your people
with an open ear
as they ascend to your dwelling
in the smoke of our offering.
We, your people,
come to celebrate sacred rites;
Look down on us beneficently.
Give us Wisdom
to do Your Will.

Please listen to us, your people.
In Your Wisdom, do not allow us to be tempted to
relinquish our ancient faith.
Give us the power to celebrate at all times
with the zeal and fidelity
You have given us.

Please listen to us, your people.

Give us the wisdom to do Your Will.
Give our warriors and our mothers strength.
We thank You in Your Wisdom
for preserving them pure.

Please listen to us, your people.
We thank you for sparing the lives of so many of your children.
Our minds are gladdened
that so many can celebrate the sacred rites
and execute Your commands.

We return thanks to
Our Mother, Earth
who sustains us.
We thank You for causing her to yield so plentifully
of her fruits.
(In the coming season, may she not withhold her fullness,
and leave any suffering for want.)

We return thanks to rivers and streams,
which run their courses upon the bosom of our mother, earth.
We thank You for supplying them with life
for our comfort and support.
(Grant that this blessing may continue.)

We return thanks to all the herbs and plants of the earth.
We thank You that in Your goodness
You have blessed them all
and given them strength to preserve our bodies healthy
and cure the diseases inflicted on us by evil spirits.
(We ask you not to take away these blessings.)
We return thanks to the Three Sisters,
Maize, Beans, Squash.
We thank You for providing them
as the main supporters of our lives.

We thank you for the abundant harvest this past season.
(We ask that the Three Sisters may never fail us
and cause our children to suffer from want.)

We return thanks to the bushes and trees
which provide us with fruit.
We thank You fro blessing them and
making them produce for the good of your creatures.
(We ask that they may not refuse to yield plentifully for our
enjoyment.)

We return thanks to the winds,
which, in moving have banished all diseases.
We thank You for so ordering.
(We ask for the continuation of this blessing.)

We return thanks to our grandfather Thunder.
We thank You for so wisely ordering the rain to descend upon
the earth,
giving us water and causing all plants to grow.
We thank You for giving us grandfather Thunder
to do Your will in protecting Your people.
(We ask you to continue this great blessing.)

We return thanks to the moon and stars
which give us light when the sun goes to rest.
We thank You for Your Wisdom
in insuring that light is never wanting to us.
(Please continue this goodness.)

We return thanks to the sun
who has looked upon the earth with a beneficent eye.
We thank You for Your unbounded Wisdom
in commanding the sun to regulate the seasons,
to dispense heat and cold,

to watch over the comfort of your people.
(Please give us the wisdom that will guide us
on the path of truth.
Keep is from all evil ways
that the sun may never hide his face from us for shame
and leave us in darkness.)

We return thanks to other spirits.
We thank You for providing us so many helpers
for our good and happiness.

Lastly,
We return thanks to You,
Our Creator and Ruler.

In You
are embodied all things.
We believe you can do no evil,
that You do all things for our good and happiness.

Should we disobey your commands,
deal not harshly with us,
but be kind to us,
as you have been to our ancestors, long gone by.

Please listen to our words
as they have ascended like the smoke.
May they be pleasing to You,
Our Creator,
the Preserver and Ruler of all things,
visible and invisible.

Na-ho.
(Amen)

(Prayer of the Iroquois Confederacy)

Jesus Christ and Forgiveness

Jesus taught the ignorant and
cured the sick of body and mind.

But the most remarkable aspect of His ministry is that
He reached out to the morally marginalized,
to those the religious establishment declared beyond hope:
prostitutes, adulterers, extortionist tax collectors,
who were collaborators with the oppressor government,
military enforcers of the government,
as well as heretics and pagans and
gluttons and drunks.

Jesus let these people touch Him
and he touched them.
He was a guest in their homes and
He ate with them.
Even more shocking,
He forgave their sins
without requiring humiliating and detailed confessions of guilt
or even firm purposes of amendment.

For this, He was castigated by religious authorities,
the guardians of public morality.
Jesus' treatment of sinners
is strange, disturbing, yet consoling.

The woman caught in adultery demonstrated
objective disorder and an intrinsically evil act.
There was no question of her guilt;
She was caught in the very act for which
Mosaic Law prescribed death by stoning.
The authorities try to implicate Jesus
for ministering to the morally marginalized
in their righteous judgment.

Jesus stoops down
and silently writes on the ground (what?) and
when asked to clarify His position says,
"Let the one among you who is without sin cast the first stone."
The convicted stoners slink away and
Jesus is left with the woman.
He does not lecture her on the sinfulness of adultery.
He does not ask her if she is guilty.
He does not even ask her if she is sorry.
Humiliation and mastery over the sinner
holds little interest for Jesus.

Jesus does not exact from her a promise or
require a firm purpose of amendment.
All Jesus says is
"Has no one condemned you? Then neither do I condemn
you."

Has Jesus confused the people?
Has Jesus confused the woman
by not clarifying the intrinsic evil of her act,
by not extracting a self-condemnation before granting forgive-
ness,
by not publicly condemning the woman as a disgrace to
Judaism?

Did Jesus undermine the moral authority of the law?
Was Jesus preference for the one who had broken the law
rather than the law's enforcement?
Was it a sign of Jesus moral weakness that
He compassionately gazed into the heart of the
frightened, suffering, marginalized woman,
rather than clinically analyzing her behavior?
Was Jesus vacillating or ambiguous about evil?

Or was His action a manifestation of the God he called
Abba or Daddy,
the God, slow to anger and boundless in kindness and com-
passion?
Has anyone through history
ever taken Jesus' action as permission to commit adultery?

Jesus forgave the woman who anointed His feet,
not because she groveled before the Pharisee host,
not because she publicly accused herself or even repented
or hated herself so much to even enter the room in the first
place
or even touch the Master.
Jesus forgave her because He was generous and compassion-
ate.
She was not forgiven because she loved;
She loved because she had been forgiven.
Are we not obliged to offer unconditional love and forgiveness,
regardless of the offenses,
because we have received God's unconditional love and
forgiveness?

Jesus invited a tax collector, a sinner, Matthew,
into His inner circle.
In doing so, He risked His own ministerial credibility
not only by associating with the morally marginalized,

but by recognizing them as partners in God's work.

Jesus said, "Those who are well do not need a Physician."
We are fortunate when we can honestly recognize ourselves
among the sinners,
as ones needing to be forgiven.
Jesus expressed moral repugnance and even contempt
for only one kind of person:
the self-righteous who condemned others from a position of
power,
those who bind heavy moral burdens for others to carry,
those who keep the minutest regulations of the law,
while driving their neighbors to self-hatred,
those who marginalize and exclude from the table,
those who they deem unworthy.

Public executions do not make the witnesses reflect.
The actions of Jesus who never encouraged
condemnation, marginalization, or humiliation,
but instead fed and clothed and cared for sinners
and even encouraged his followers to lay down their lives for
others,
force us to reflect on our ministry
and to bring our actions and lives in harmony
with Jesus' call to forgive.

Path

Do I embark on a journey
which has an unknown destination?

Do I embark on a journey
which has an unclear destination?

We go through life
taking paths
leading to destinations we envision.
We go through life
in search of destinations,
taking paths
we think lead us to them.

In fact,
none of our journeys
lead to destinations of certainty.
Most of the paths we take
lead to unexpected places.

The destination is not
what it's all about.
The lessons are on the journey.
The pebbles of Wisdom are on the path.
In focusing on a destination,

I miss the Wisdom nuggets.

If I only took paths with certain destinations,
I'd never move.
If I only began journeys leading me
where I wanted,
I'd not take the first step.

When the Holy Spirit calls,
I must move.
I must have trust in God.
I must go forward,
Not knowing where the path leads
And
Not needing to know.

Justice and Mercy

Interesting
How we demand Justice
when we are injured.

We want
Accountability, Restitution, Punishment.
We will not consider Forgiveness
unless there is
Admission of Guilt, Repentance, Firm Purpose of Amendment.

Many of us have been taught that
God acts the same way;
That God will not forgive us unless
We admit our wrongs, Express sorrow, Vow never to sin again,
and
Make a perfect–or at worst, an imperfect–Act of Contrition.
We have been taught that God's forgiveness is dependent
on us doing all the right things.

Strange,
Christ didn't seem to live that way.
Time after time after time,
Jesus forgave
without condemnation, without humiliation, without
marginalization.

Time after time after time,
Jesus forgave
without asking if the person were guilty or sorry or repentant.

(Perhaps Repentance is not a requirement for Forgiveness,
but the only appropriate response to it.)

The prodigal son's Loving Father
began the celebration the moment he saw his son up the road,
having no idea if his son was sorry or repentant.

Jesus never asked the adulterous woman
if she were sorry;
And He did not condemn her, nor humiliate her, nor lecture
her.

Time after time after time,
Jesus ate with the morally marginalized,
never first requiring them to express sorrow and apology.

Jesus seems to embody a Godly
Love and forgiveness
Freely Given.

Do we have it all wrong?
We spend our lives seeking God's Forgiveness,
which is freely available,
When we should be spending our lives–like Jesus,
freely sharing that gift with others.

Role of the Laity

The role of the laity?
Simple.
To fully serve the needs of each other
using our God-given skills, talents, gifts.

What did we do before we organized
a full-time professional clergy
to do it for us?
We did it all ourselves.

Let's look to the original lay team of
Jesus Christ and the apostles and disciples.
They served the needs of those around them
with Love and Compassion.
Christ's Servant Leadership was
non-bureaucratic, disruptive, and
inclusive.
Jesus walked his talk;
He showed the role of the laity
by his life.
It was full of Love and Compassion
manifested in Forgiveness.
Could it be any clearer?
Could it be any simpler?
(Simple, perhaps, but not easy.)

What is there in Community (Parishes)
that we laity cannot do for each other?
Across the world,
Lay people are
ministering to the physical, emotional, and spiritual needy,
teaching, preaching, administrating,
forgiving and blessing one another.
The gifts are given; they need to be brought from under the
bushel basket.

For too long we have abandoned our responsibilities
to the clergy;
the Holy Spirit is awakening the need for us to re-assume
them,
once again, to be servant leaders.

Need we let the shrinking cadre of professional clergy
keep the Sacraments or the sacraments from people?
The role of the laity?

WWJD?

Reflection

When turbulent
and in a frenzy,
the lake's waves and whitecaps
prevent reflection.

The lake best reflects heaven
when still
and
calm
and
silent.

Spiritual Leadership

In times past,
Spiritual Leaders of a Community
came from the Community.
Priests, Deacons, Presbyters, Pastors,
and even Bishops
were Of the Community which they led.

They were chosen and nominated
and accepted by their own people.
When the Community deemed that a change was needed,
The Community initiated a change.

Along the way,
People, parishioners
yielded that right.
Bishops were given the authority,
to go far beyond mere ordination.
They were yielded the power
to assign and re-assign Pastoral Leadership
regardless of the wishes of the
Community.
No longer were Pastoral Leaders
Of the Community
which they led.
St. Luke's has been Blessed.

First with Sister Celine,
who although not originally from our Community,
has become one of us.
Second with Sister Kathy,
who is of our Community.

The same cannot said of Sacramental Ministers.
The swinging doors of Diocesan whim
has paraded numerous persons through.
The turnstiles of Diocesan administration
has given and taken away no-one who has become
Of St. Luke's Community.

A famous man said,
"People get the kind of Government they deserve."
Do people get the kind of Sacramental Minister we deserve?
When we acquiesce,
Do say, "It's what we deserve?"

Lord's Prayer

Oh Loving Creator
who lives in all of us,
We are in awe of your greatness!
Your presence is here;
Your Love is demonstrated
in our lives
through You.
Provide us today
the opportunity to meet our needs.
Forgive us for
rejecting and oppressing others
as we forgive those
who reject and oppress us.
Do not let us fall into self-doubt.
Preserve the dignity of
this Community.
For Yours is
Truth,
Empowerment, and
Celebration
Forever and ever.
Hooray!

Love is

God breathed me to life,
God sustains me with each breath,
God lives within me.

In choosing *My* way,
I isolate me from God within,
I prefer *My* plan.

Separate from God,
I cannot Love, nor be Loved,
I am without Love.

True Love is: Clearing
a path to God within me,
within everyone.

Loving God within,
I Love all God's creation,
including my self.

I can Love others
who have not found God within
and cannot accept Love.

My God-path open,

I can be Loved by others,
I can accept Love.

When others Love me,
their Love empowers me
with God's energy.

When I Love others,
we are each energized as
God's Love flows through me.

In Loving and Loved,
I am united with all,
with God living in us.

In Loving and Loved,
We are united with God,
all living in God.

When we live in love,
we live in God,
and God in us.
(1 John 4, 7-16)

A Loving Connection

Safe enough to share intense feelings
Respectful
Space to tell one's story
Patience to go below the surface
Willingness to look for role models
Responsibility for behavior
Awareness of Consequences
Filled with Laughter at ourselves
Appreciation and Joy
Self analysis and description
Intrigue about behavior–success and failure
Excitement about discovery
Acceptance of negative feelings and a willingness to let them
go
Observer self
Knowledge of what is and is not within control
Promptness, attentiveness, responsiveness
Realization that choices are necessary
Problems addressed with hope and patience
Genuineness
Practical
Clarity
Wisdom sharing
Silence and solitude
Discarding of hidden no-longer-relevant rules limiting freedom

New approaches to life
Step back
Negative experiences as lessons
Patience, low expectations with high hopes
Preciousness of life
Human value
Infectious passion and courage
Awareness of self-feelings
Humor or hope to integrate failures and losses into wisdom
Enjoyment of the fruits of profound experiences
Reasonable distance
Boundaries
Replacing projections with peace, composure, and gratitude
Review
Helpful responses without pressure
Adults, not child and parent, student and teacher
Balance
Oneness with nature
Appreciation of life's gifts
Self-acceptance
Summarization
Mirror
Journal
Reframing

Merely Survive or Grow?

Don't merely try
To make the best of your situation;

Work to let your situation
Make the best of you!

My Circular Mantra

God is Love; I Love; I am One with God is . . .
(A never ending mantra)

God is Love; I Love; I am One with God is . . .
(I acknowledge God's existence as my creator.)

God is Love; I Love; I am One with God is . . .
(God is manifested in life as love.)

God is Love; I Love; I am One with God is . . .
(God loves me; thirsts for me.)

God is Love; **I Love**; I am One with God is . . .
(The call to Christianity is a call to love all, unconditionally.)

God is Love; **I Love; I** am One with God is . . .
(It must start with me; I must see myself as loveable.)

God is Love; I Love; **I am** One with God is . . .
(I exist for love.)

God is Love; I Love; **I am One with God** is . . .
(In love, I live in God and God in me; we are united.)

God is Love; I Love; I am One with God is . . . etc.
(This says it all for me.)

Me

Define an narrow me,
you starve yourself of me
and you.

Nail me down in a box of cold words,
that box is a coffin.

I do not know who I am.
I am in astounding lucid confusion.

I do not belong to the land or
to any known or unknown sea.

Although she nurtures me,
Mother Earth cannot claim me.

My birthplace is not Chicago;
It is placelessness.

You see my mouth, ears, eyes, nose–
they are not me.

I am in life, of life, life.
I am of all times, all worlds.
So are you.

Listen!
Listen to who is speaking in you,
in me.
Admit it and change everything.

Our voices echo
off the walls of God.

Moment

Each moment in our life
is precious,
is special.

We enjoy so few of them,
by focusing on
those past or
those to come.

Each moment of our life
should be en-joyed,
should be celebrated.
Each moment's passing
calls for reflection.

Is the moment
23:59, 12/31/99
more special than any other?
Is the moment
00:01, 01/01/00
more important than any other?

Perhaps only because
so many of us
will not be in the past

or in the future,
but in that
Present Moment.

Mind

For much of my life,
I worshiped at the altar of
the thinking mind.

Much of my journey
was devoted to
the acquisition of knowledge
and
information
and
things.

Seeing the world
and myself
through the filter of
the information and knowledge
I had gathered,
I became imprisoned by
the ideas and images I pursued.

I thought I knew myself.

All I knew was what I thought about myself.

When I thought

I knew the world around me,
I was barred from
seeing the mystery
held within each moment.

Moving Out to Get In

When I am drunk on myself,
a friend often seems a thorn;
When I am able to leap out of myself,
I become friend.

When drunk on myself,
I am prey to mosquitos;
When free of myself,
I can hunt elephants.

When I am drunk on myself,
I am locked in a cloud of grief;
When I leap out of myself,
the moon catches me and holds me in its arms.

When drunk on myself,
friends scatter;
When free of myself,
friendship is full of brilliance and dazzle.

When I am drunk on myself,
I am withered autumn leaves;
When I leap out of myself,
Winter appears in the dazzling robes of spring.

Searching for quiet,
I find disquiet;
Through disquiet,
I suddenly find quiet.

Scavenging for delicacies
brings distaste;
Not needing them
renders all delicious.

Hunting for satisfaction,
brings only disappointment;
Being sated with what is,
rolls pearls of joy to my feet.

When I am passionate for
a friends tyranny and not tenderness;
My arrogance turns me to
a lover that weeps.

When I am drunk on myself,
I know not me;
When I can leap out of myself,
I begin to find the true me.

My Call to Awareness

Everything I see
has its roots in the unseen world.
The forms may change,
yet the essence remains the same.
Every wonderful sight I see
will vanish;
Every sweet word will fade.

But I am not disheartened.
The source from which they come
is eternal and growing,
branching out,
giving new life and new joy.

I do not weep.
The source is within me
and the whole world is springing from it.
The source is full
and its waters are ever-flowing.

I do not grieve, I drink my fill.
It will never run dry,
this endless ocean of Love.

From the moment I came into the world,

a mountain was in front of me,
that I might climb it.

From earth I became plant,
from plant, I became animal,
then I became human being
endowed with
mind, heart, gut.

I am in awe of my body, born of dust,
how perfect it is.
I do not fear its end.
I was never less by dying.
When I pass beyond human form,
I will soar the heavens
and then plunge into the vast ocean of consciousness.

The drop of water that is me
will become a hundred mighty seas.
But the drop not only becomes the ocean,
the ocean, too, becomes the drop.

Present Moment

Reading in bed,
I came across the line,
"Everything you will ever need,
is available to you
in the present moment."

Wow!
Powerful!

As I pondered it for some moments,
I began to see moments of my past life
flash before me
very very clearly
as if on video tape.
And I saw the events
in minute detail,
detail which I had long forgotten–
or never noticed before!

This *video* randomly played back for me
many many events
from all parts of my life,
my childhood,
my teen-age years,
high school, college,

early marriage,
career, etc.

Wow!
I was enthralled.
It was marvelous to be able to
relive so much of my life.

I wondered if I could control the sequence,
choose the events,
And I did!!!
I picked whatever event I wanted to see again,
and there it was!
In detail!
And in full clarity.

I was in a sweat.

Then all of a sudden,
Splat!
All of these video screens,
all of the replays of my life
were up on a wall in back of me
all playing at the same time.
All of the past events of my past life
were all being replayed at the same time
on a wall in back of me.

My heart was pounding
ready to burst from my chest.
What of the future, I thought.

So I turned away from the wall in back of me
and looked forward
and there in front of me behind

what seemed to be plexiglass
was the galaxy,
the cosmos,
the universe,
millions, billions of stars and planets and constellations.

I was awestruck.

Then, slowly,
the wall of my past pushed me forward
into the plexiglass
squeezing me tighter and tighter and tighter
till I could not breath,
and then,

I exploded

and joined all the stars and constellations
and was one with the cosmos.

Then,
there I was reading my book again,
"Everything I will ever need"
available to me
right now,
in the present moment.

God's way of trying to show me
there is no past,
there is no future
only now?

Myths

Myths never were,
but
Always are.

Myths are the foundations for
Real Moral Values.

Myths:

Not falsehoods of the world
told by primitives,
but
A True Story
about the workings of God
in the human Soul
told by Geniuses.

There is nothing in the world truer
than
Myth.

Without Myth,
people dis-integrate.

Napoleon on St. Helena

I know men;
Jesus Christ was no mere man.

Some see his resemblance to
founders of empires
and the gods of other religions.
That resemblance
belies the truth.
One cannot compare Christ
with any other.

Christ's empire,
his march across the ages and the realms
is an insoluble mystery.

Jesus Christ.
What a conqueror!
He controls humanity at will
and wins to himself not a nation,
but the whole human race.
Marvel!

Somehow, he attaches to himself
the human soul.
How?

By a miracle which surpasses all miracles:
He claims the Love of men,
the human heart,
the most difficult thing in the world to obtain,
something the wisest man cannot force from his truest friend,
something no father can compel from his children,
no wife from her husband,
no brother his brother,
no sister from her sister.

He claims the human heart.
He requires it absolutely,
undividedly.
And
He obtains it.

Alexander, Caesar, Hannibal, Louis XIV
strove in vain to secure this.
They conquered the world

yet, they had not a single friend,
or at least
they have none now.

Christ speaks
and from that moment
all generations belong to him.
and
they are joined to him
much more closely
than by ties of blood
and
by a much more intimate, sacred, and powerful
Communion.

Jesus kindles the flame of Love
which causes self to die
and
this Love triumphs over all.
The founders of religions
had not the least conception of this
Mystic Love
which forms the essence of Christianity.

I, Napoleon,
have filled multitudes with enough passion and devotion
to be willing to suffer death for me.
But the enthusiasm of my soldiers
can not hold a candle to
Christian Love.
They are as unalike
as their causes.

My presence,
my electric glance,
my voice,
kindled fire in hearts.
I took the sentiments of men
by storm
But I was not able to communicate that power
to anyone.
None of my generals ever learned it from me.
Moreover,
I do not possess the secret
of perpetuating
a Love for me in the hearts of others forever.

I languish here at St. Helena,
chained upon this rock.
Who fights; who conquers for me?

Who thinks of me?
Who has remained true to me?
This is my fate
and the fate of all great men.
We are forgotten and
my name and the names of all the world's mightiest conquerors
and most illustrious emperors
soon become only the subject of a schoolboy's task.
What an abyss
between my profound misery
and the eternal reign of Jesus Christ
who is preached, Loved, worshiped,
and
lives on throughout the world.
Nations pass,
thrones crumble,
But Christ's empire remains–
in the hearts of men,
on into eternity.

Need

Often, in need of Love,
we are so drawn
to one we think can
give us the love we need,
we are driven to try
to possess her,
to possess him.

Even though we know
that this seeming lover
cannot be possessed,
we crave all of them,
all of their attention.
We want to give them all the love they need.

But no human can give us all the love we need;
We can provide no one all the love they need.

And in fact,
if we follow this drive to possess,
we kill love,
we stop growth,
we drive our loved-one away.

For the opposite of love

is not hate,
but fear
and
Control.
True Love grows only in Freedom.
In control,
love dies.

When we try to possess
the one we love,
to control her or him,
we stop growth,
we end love,
we drive them away,
we lose the very one we desired to possess.

Oh, No

Reading a book on
"Sharing Wisdom,"

I came across
an old Spanish proverb:

"Tell me what you brag about
and
I'll tell you what you lack."

I read on
believing that it did not apply to me
as I was not prone to brag.

But, it would not let me go on reading;
It pulled me back to it
no matter how hard I tried to leave it behind.
It said,
"This applies to you, John."

I tried to think about any bragging.

I often expressed thankfulness
at being so blessed in life,
but it was not bragging and

I lacked no essentials in life.

And then it hit me.
Like a ton of bricks!

I often bragged, yes, bragged
about overflowing with Love of others.

"Tell me what you brag about
and
I'll tell you what you lack"
it read.

So much Love for others,
yet lacking it myself?

Old Man Winter

Old man winter and I
are much the same.
And not just because
we're into whites and greys.

We both try to gain attention
by blowing hard
and sometimes icing down.

We let everyone know
we need no one
and they better pay us heed
because
we can affect their plans.

Despite our ferocity,
we can be beautiful;
despite our noise,
we can be peaceful;
despite our exterior harshness,
we are really soft and gentle.

Old man winter and I;
some despise us,
run away in fear,

but many have fun with us,
enjoy us,
especially the kids.

To may we represent an end,
to a year, to life;
to others wisdom,
for in our darkness and solitude and tranquility
is true self
and
God.

Old man winter and I,
respect us, fear us, enjoy us,
whatever;
we both will be gone in time
giving way to
Spring and new life.

But
we both have left our marks on creation
and
Winter is simply a forerunner to Spring.

Open Table

Jesus broke the laws
and
Shared meals with sinners.

He never condoned sin
but
Jesus always opened the door to sinners
Unconditionally.

We gather round the Eucharistic table,
not because we are saints with VIP tickets,
but because we are sinners and
hunger for God's mercy and compassion.

What Would Jesus Do
if He saw today how we use
the Eucharistic Table
to divide the "good" from the "bad",
to exclude the "unworthy?"

Jesus broke bread with
the poor, the outcast, prostitutes, tax collectors and sinners.

The barriers we now place around the Eucharistic Table
may be the worst heresy of our day.

We have made access to the nourishing, merciful love of Jesus
conditional.
In doing so,
We have stolen God's mercy from the heart of sinners.

The Eucharist,
The sacrament of God's merciful loving presence
is celebrated in thanksgiving that
we all form the body of Christ.

When we celebrate it
while underhandedly conditioning the mercy of God,
we profane the body and blood of Our Lord.

Candidates for sainthood
have no need to receive the Eucharist,
but it is the self-righteous who build the barriers and
judge others unfit
to approach the table of the Lord.

WWJD

Order

The need for order in my life
causes me heartache.

I want everything to be
the way I want it to be.

I want my children to have good lives,
even better than mine.
But I have no control over that
and must let them
face what they must face,
be who they must be.
I can help,
I can pray,
but it's their journeys.

I expect people to be
the way I want people to be.
But,
people do not behave as I wish.
I know that is true,
so why does it frustrate me so
when they are not as I wish?

Having good intentions,

doing the right things,
I expect events to happen
as I expect them to happen.
But events are not in my control.
I can do what I do well
and with good intention,
but events are also affected
by other than me.

So why does it upset me so when
I cannot find the order I seek?

I know that true Faith
is being comfortable in uncertainty
yet I seek certainty
in people and events.

Is it a lack of Faith?

The disciples sent out two by two
were told to take nothing with them.

Maybe on my journey,
I'm just trying to take too much with me.

Paradox

I only began to know myself
when I went outside myself
to learn about others.

I only began to feel love
when I gave love
helping others.

I only began to live
when I was willing to die to myself
in service of others.

I only began to be me
when I accepted others
as they are.

I only began to truly know my faith
when I began to live my faith
serving others.

I only began to climb life's mountain
when I helped others
who had stumbled.

I only began to see

when I gave up
the need to see.

I only began to find God within
when I found God
in others.

I only began to feel forgiven
when I forgave others
for everything.

An ever-changing past

All of my past experiences are part of me.

Do these past experiences
remain fixed?
(Always thought they did.)

Or
do they change
in relation to
who I am now?
(Huh)

Do my past experiences change
as I change
with each new experience?

If each new experience in my life
is simply the overturning and the putting in place
another piece of the picture puzzle which makes up my life
picture,
then each piece (previously exposed) does change
in relation to the total picture.

Maybe, the past
is not canned, static, complete, over, fixed.

Perhaps, the past
is fluid and ever-changing
more so even than
the future, which does not exist
or
the present which simply is.

Maybe,
with each new experience in life,
I need to go back and re-examine the past
to see how it has changed
(in relation to my new now)
and
to learn what new lessons it holds
for me now.

Maybe the most sacred function of memory
is to render the distinction between past, present, and future
meaningless.

Maybe our challenge is
to inhabit in the now
the same eternity that God inhabits.

Path

How can I know I'm on the right path
when I can't see any path at all?

If I admit I don't know where I'm going,
I won't be lost.

Paths

A long way from the beginning of our climb
up the mountain of life,
our paths
come together, cross, intertwine, merge
for awhile.

And so,
We help each other on this part of our journey.
We let our light shine on each other's path
to help guide us.
You trip and fall; I help you up.
I stumble, you keep me from falling.
I scrape my knee, you help me heal.
You face stumbling blocks I help you convert to
stepping stones.

Each of our paths remains uniquely ours,
but we need each other
along the way.

We offer each a hand when hanging on
by our fingernails.
And
We keep each other from falling into the trap
of stopping the climb

in a wayside inn or cabin.
We challenge each other
to keep on climbing,
to keep on growing.

Neither of us sees the end,
the peak, the pinnacle.
But we know it's there
we must go.

The cloud of the unknowing
keeps us both from seeing
our ultimate goal.
But we know
the Love we give and receive from each other
pierces that cloud
coming from God
while guiding us to God.

So together we climb
Unique and United
in Love.

Paul

*Many praised me
for protecting the Law and Tradition
by searching out those who would divide the people
by their belief in He who claimed to be Messiah.
*The praise seemed to make the effort worthwhile.

The blaze of light filled the countryside
and felled me to the ground.
I was paralyzed and confused.
*I opened my eyes–to darkness!
*I could not see.

*Thus, I began my journey
*to an inner vision of profound reality.
I was stripped of my self-sufficiency
and forced to depend on others,
*to enter a new form of relationship with them.
*I was no longer proud, capable, sure.

*I was intelligent and well-educated,
*but it was not by brilliant reasoning that I began to grasp the
Truth
that Jesus is the eternal expression of the Living God.
*It was the overwhelming experience of God
*first through inner revelation,

*then through the community of believers.
*My Faith was actualized both
*by the voice of the Spirit within me and
*His reaching me through others.
*I learned those is no separation in these realities.
*I became united with the Word of God within me and
all of my actions were enclosed in that circle of light.
*I was at first terrified
*but all I was given made power, adulation, security, and
respect
*seem like rubbish.

*I had been immersed in my role
*and forgot my true identity.
When forced to be dependent on those whom I was persecut-
ing
*I had no choice but to be myself.
*Only when I was able to stop projecting my own pride
*and my self-righteousness,
*could I find myself, my true self.
*And once others got to know the true me,
*they trusted me and their attitude toward me changed
*because my attitude changed.
*As I got to know and accept my true self,
*I was able to be open and honest with all I met.

*I learned that Christ is in God and
*I am in Him and He in me.

(*applies to me as well as St. Paul)

Pendulum

In order to avoid pain and sorrow
at one extreme in my life,

I can let the pendulum of life
stay motionless in the middle.

But,
In avoiding the pain and sorrow at one end of the arc,
I miss all the joys and ecstasies at the other end.

Not worth it,
and besides,

A clock whose pendulum stays motionless
is rather useless.

Pentecost

Isn't the coming of the Holy Spirit into our lives
what it's all about?

We can pray to God
and
We can tell the story of Jesus, but
without an active relationship with the Holy Spirit,
isn't religion a dead language,
a remembrance of things past?

The true Christian story
is not about our glorious past;
It is about the present and
the promise for eternity.
Grace is happening now.

Grace happens because
The Holy Spirit lives in us.

The Spirit cannot be taught,
only caught.
The Spirit comes to us
in relationship and
try as we may,
We cannot reduce it to a formula.

The disciples lives were changed,
blown open by divine invitation.
Pentecost is a feast of understanding.
They had followed Jesus for years,
heard everything,
witnessed miracles,
knew His miracles,
cringed at His crucifixion,
rejoiced as His resurrection,
and still did not understand 50 days after Easter.
They had every benefit we might wish,
but still did not understand.

The Spirit opened the window for
those hanging around in the upper room
to let in the light and air.
The Spirit opened their minds
and for the first time, they saw.
They stumbled out onto the street and
proclaimed what they saw and heard and
baptized 3000 that day!

The Holy Spirit circles the globe,
finds people who's hearts are open
and who's lives are ready,
taking up residence there.

The dead giveaway is
the spirit of understanding that envelopes
the person in whom the Holy Spirit lives.

The Holy Spirit breathes on us,
offering us peace.
No roaring wind,
just a gentle breath.

No pyrotechnics,
just a relationship we can trust.
The Spirit
imparted in a quiet moment.

The point is to
Get Pentecost!
Be ready for the Holy Spirit.
Anticipate it.
Pray for it.
It is necessary for our lives as people of faith.

Maybe our lives will change dramatically or
maybe we'll just
"get it."
Whichever,
there is enough Pentecost for everybody.

Pentecost 2

Pentecost completes the mission of Jesus.
Our salvation is achieved
within a human earthly setting
by a Divine Agent, Jesus Christ,
working through
The Power of the Holy Spirit.

Wind, water, fire are striking symbols of
God's Holy Spirit.

Pentecost is a feast of Liberation and Freedom,
sometimes achieved with pain and in suffering.
Sometimes, the Spirit's presence is recognized
only in life's breaking points,
the moments when
our lives seem to come unglued.

Pentecost is feast of unity, a celebration of peace
in the midst of our ever-present
anxieties, antipathies, and tensions.

The Gift of the Holy Spirit:

Is given to ALL people,
("They were all filled with the Holy Spirit.")

not just Bishops and Priests,
not just those of one religion.

Is a gift of Unity,
("They were all with one accord in one place.")
The Spirit makes the many to be One
in the Body of Christ.
The Holy Spirit reverses the human condition
started at the tower of Babel.
Individuals are transformed into
persons capable of relating to one another.
The Spirit brings Unity and mutual comprehension.
("They were one in mind and heart.")

Is a gift of Diversity,
given to each directly.
The Spirit makes us, not only One,
but also different.
At Pentecost, various languages were not abolished,
but they ceased to be a cause of division.
We are called
to realize the distinctive characteristics
of our individual personality.
Each of us is called
to be unique.

Picture Window

Looking out at Torch Lake
and beyond,
I am simply looking at
God's canvas.

Through this picture window,
moment by moment,
brush stroke by brush stroke,
God paints for me
and ever-changing
world of beauty.

Each moment,
God presents to me a painting,
which has never been seen before,
and which shall never be seen again.

I add each of them to my soul's collection
simply by stopping,
by seeing,
by rejoicing.

Plan

"Plan your work;
Work your plan."

This was the motto of
my life in commerce.

"Identify with results;
No surprises."

This is what makes
a successful business executive.

Now, I'm learning
that it's not my plan I can work,
but only the Divine.

And how can I identify with results?
I don't control them.
God does.
I can only give my best effort.

And no surprises?
No surprises?
No surprises?

Creation is full of surprise.

A word that best typifies God
is
Surprise.

I enjoy surprise.

Successful executive?
Maybe.

But God does not call me to success,
only to service.
only to best efforts,
only to Love,

only to be comfortable in and enjoy

Divine Surprise.

The Power

I sense that
while everything is always changing,
always growing,
always dying,

There is underlying all this change
A living Power
that is changeless.

This Power
holds everything together,
Creating, Dissolving, Re-creating.

This Power
is
God
and
since nothing else I see through my senses
escapes demise,

God alone is.

Is the Power good or bad?
I see it as purely Good.
For I can see that

In the midst of death, life persists,
In the midst of falsehood, truth persists,
In the midst of pain and sorrow, healing and comfort persist,
In the midst of darkness, light persists.

(from Gandi)

Stop Pretending

The blind practice of ritual
as holy behavior
is as old as
religion itself.

We do pious impersonations
to impress God,
to impress others,
first parents,
then children.

Then,
we judge others
bu their willingness to conform
to our pious behaviors.

How easily we recite
our creeds,
our prayers.
How easily we affirm our Faith in words
and
yet how quickly
we refuse the challenge and suffering of
true discipleship.

Life's greatest trials
test our Faith
and
expose holes in
our understanding of God.

A bended knee
is so much easier
than
an truly open heart.

Puzzle

My life seems like a picture puzzle,
made up of millions of pieces,
initially all face down on God's table.

Slowly, moment by moment,
each piece is turned over and
revealed to me.

As the pieces are exposed
and put into place
a picture—my picture-begins to form.

In time,
I begin to see how all the pieces are related and
Out of the apparent chaos in front of me,
a beautiful picture begins to take shape.

As the puzzle pieces of my life
are connected,
I see that

Every piece—light and dark—is required,
No piece is missing,
and
There are no extra pieces.

Quest

When I finally got off the treadmill
going nowhere
and
when I let go of the control
I never had
nor
would have
and when I got back into the moment,
into the now,
I shivered with cold
and
with fright.

I discovered
that
I did not know myself,
only what I thought about myself.

But then,
God rushed in,
warm loving God.

God's passion
made me glow with heat
and

I held my head and hands high
and
I yelled,

"God is Love!"

I laughed with tears
and
the things I feared
curled up
like burnt paper.

Questions

My anxiety and insecurity
come from being afraid
to ask the right questions

because I might not have the answers.

I huddle with others
in the pale light of insufficient answers
to questions
we are too afraid to ask.

Reflection

I looked into the windless lake,
saw my clear reflection,
and thought it was me.

Then, the wind,
beyond my control,
came and sent ripples, even waves,
across the lake,
changing, distorting the reflection
so I could no longer see myself
in the lake.

All my life,
my family, my career, my possessions
were a reflection of me
and I thought it was me.
But the winds of life
(or was it the Holy Spirit)
beyond my control
came and changed it all
and they no longer reflected me
and I could no longer clearly see myself
in them.

And I discovered that

my real self could not be held in a reflection,
but only deep within myself.

Thank God for the wind.
(Holy Spirit?)

Risk

The flight outside the cocoon
is fraught with risks.

But to never have flown
in order to avoid those risks;
Tragedy!

The caterpillar also dies.

Sacramental Moment

At liturgy one weekday morning in Lancaster Pennsylvania,
a reading from the First Letter of John
exploded in me!

It described and defined Love as God is Love.
It spoke to
Living in Love
as
Living in God
and
God living in us.

I began reading it daily
seeing that it contained the answers to
all my questions,
and maybe,
all the questions of the world.
It became part of my daily prayers.

And as I prayed it each day,
I gained new insights
to each line.

I had begun recording my insights
when I kept getting the feeling that

I should somehow share these insights.

Several years after the initial experience,
I was attending a weeknight
Communion Service at St. Luke's Church in Northern
Michigan,
when the scheduled Lector (reader) did not show up
and I was asked to sub.

I had not had a chance to prepare as I usually do as Lector,
but stepped up to the lectern relying on the Holy Spirit for
help.
The passage took my breath away;
It was my reading from the First Letter of John!

After a pause to catch my breath,
I began proclaiming the message
without needing to view the lectionary.
It had been my daily prayer for years;
Who needed a lectionary.
Needless to say,
the congregation was awestruck.
How was John able to proclaim this reading
without reading it?

With heart beating twice normal
and perspiration dripping from my forehead,
I explained the whole situation
to the congregation.

I don't remember much of the Service that followed;
I kept thinking about what had happened
and what it meant.
It was clearly a message from the Holy Spirit
for me to

keep on keeping on, John.

After that night,
I formalized my writeup of the passage,
put it into a little booklet,
ran copies,
and began distributing them
to family, friends and whoever
the Holy Spirit so moved me.
I have given out nearly 1000 copies so far.

In addition,
I prepared a workshop (seminar) entitled
"Love is the Answer, Whatever the Question."
and offer it to churches and religious groups.

The reading has helped change my life,
and perhaps the lives of others,
and
Twice more (at random),
I have been scheduled to Lector
The First Letter of John, 4, 7-16.

Coincidence: God's way of remaining anonymous.

Sadness

Sadness is but one note
on the scale of Joy.

Regret has to do with *then*. It is out of time.
Regret is about something that I am powerless to change,
yet when I hold on to it, I am trying to change something
I cannot.

I must accept that which I cannot change.
I may not like it, but I must accept it.
When I accept it, I can release it.
If I do not, I am stuck in regret,
in the past,
which no longer exists.

I am trying to live in the moment,
to be with what is now.
At this moment,
all is well.

My anxieties are about the future.
Somehow when they get to the present moment,
I handle them.
Stuck in regret, I am disempowered and debilitated.
In regret, I am crippled and impaired and

unable to take positive actions,
thus depriving myself of self-esteem.

Regret is self-criticism
that gains energy from others' sympathy and pity.
Others feeling sorry for me
encourages me to believe in the power of what was.

I must be at home with what is,
so that what might be,
can be.

When can I be joyful?

If not, now,
When?

Sailing through Life

Sailing my boat
is like living my life.

In sailing, as in life,
I am aware of my relationship with the elements
over which I have no control.
To presume dominion over them
is as futile in life as in sailing.

I am not pitted against any others in sailing,
only myself,
as in life.

Following my passion and dreams by sailing
helps me to learn to
follow my dreams, nurture them, cling to them.
As sailing transforms me,
so do my dreams and my passion.

Climbing the wind, my boat teaches me
to be at home in the world of free moral judgement.
Not setting my course by some fixed mark on shore teaches me
not to live by dogma or edict.
I know that those who are rigid
finish last and have the least joy.

In sailing there is no destination;
It is all about the journey.
In sailing, the wind tells me what to do,
in life, the Holy Spirit.

In sailing, it's all about relationships;
Wind, water, boat, sail, sailor.
In life, I grow in my humanity
in relationships.
As I am linked to the makers of my boat and my sails,
so am I linked to my ancestors.

Tacking teaches me
patience and fortitude and
to recognize the journey's obstacles;
The wind is not always at my back.
Whatever I'm enjoying now or fighting now
will change.

Tacking too often or
staying on a tack too long
teaches me that
each change in direction in life
requires adjustment.
Tacking, if not handled fluidly, loses momentum
in sailing and in life.
Life is tack upon tack upon tack.

Momentum is critical in sailing
as in life.
Without momentum, I hang in irons.
With momentum, I can change my tack and
regain control.
To try and change without it is ineffectual,
dooms me to be a prisoner of the wind.

The only way to come about
is to maintain momentum on my present tack,
and not change too quickly.
Without wind in my sails,
I'm at the mercy of others.

Running with the wind can be dangerous,
can lead to an accidental jibe.
Sometimes a 350 degree turn
is better than one of ten degrees.
A jibe caused by inadvertence or heedlessness
can be fatal.
The wind at my back
makes the journey deceptively easy,
lulls me into a false sense of security.
My security is in me
when I am vigilant.
I need to watch my sails, the signs of wind around me,
and an accidental jibe.

When the winds are good,
when things are favorable,
I tend to think they'll stay that way.
Then comes the calm.
Can do nothing in the calm,
but relax and enjoy it.
The wind cannot change 180 degrees
without stopping first.
Sailing teaches me to use the calms
in life
to contemplate the new wind,
a change in direction.

If the wind changes,
I cannot expect to keep doing the same things

and stay on course;
If circumstances change in life,
I cannot expect to continue doing the same things
and stay on course.

Fretting about a future trouble
takes my mind off sailing now
placing me in jeopardy now.
Fretting about a future risk
consumes energy now.
I need to approach a danger
before I know it's real.

Fog confuses.
I move without knowing where for sure.
I need to let go of the tiller,
try not to control.
I learn to distrust anyone
who knows for certain.

In fog,
I learn to wait for the wind,
trust in the Holy Spirit,
let the breath of God guide me.
The fog does clear
when the Spirit blows.

My boat is forgiving.
My centerboard warns me of shallows.
My sails alert me to wind changes.
My boat comes back upright.
Like my boat,
I must be forgiving,
return upright
after a blow.

Each wind is unique.
I must be at one with whatever wind blows.
I cannot traverse the globe but
I can thrive on the gusts I am given
or relax in a calm.
I learn to live the moment that is,
to savor the sounds of the wind and waves
or lack of them.

Losing my rudder puts me at the mercy of wind and waves.
To be free, I need a direction.
A direction followed with passion
gives my life meaning.
O must never lose my rudder.

The wind's direction?
True or apparent?
In part, it's up to me.
I've got to be me.

I did not, could not,
force my sons to learn to sail
or live life fully.
I introduced them to each,
let them taste my passion for each,
blessed them and
set them free.
They sail
as they sail.

To sail,
I must be unattached.
Attached, I would never leave the dock.
I must be free to sail.
In life, also.

Sailing teaches me Life teaches me.

Self

I gain meaning only in relation to others.

I cannot truly "be" by myself.

I am like one piece of a huge picture puzzle.
Alone, I am meaningless,
odd shaped and with no reference.

In right relation to the other pieces of the puzzle (universe),
I gain meaning.
I am necessary to complete the picture and
Without me, the picture is incomplete.
I relate to those around me and
to all others in the total.

I am meaningful in relation to all others,
including all my ancestors and
all future generations.

The piece of the puzzle
that has fallen to the floor
must be picked up and
placed in right relation to the other pieces
in order to give it meaning and
to complete the picture.

That piece,
without meaning alone,
is needed to complete the picture and
to give me meaning.

I can only inter-be.

Shadows

I had looked for achievements, success, possessions
to bring light into my life.
I looked to the future,
to the attainment of accomplishments
as the key to my wholeness,
as if it were somewhere else.

As I focused on my own self interest,
it left me feeling
unsatisfied, misdirected, shallow.
The insecurity flowing from these feelings
led to blame, control, self-protection, and hostility.
I often tried to anesthetize myself to these feelings,
but that only served to increase my isolation, my separateness.
In the darkness,
I found myself longing for
some ideal future,
some miraculous formula
to make me whole.

I learned that
to fully live,
I needed to find light
amid the darkness,
that I needed to help others heal,

and thus,
begin to heal myself.
Living in peace
requires
great Love.
I had to be willing
not to turn away from, not to shun
the shadows,
but to turn toward them.

In taking that first step,
I began to cast away fears, doubts, despair.
I found that darkness is not my opponent;
rejection and denial of it is.

In life's difficulties,
I must do as St. John of the Cross says,
"If a person wishes to be sure of the road they tread upon,
they must close their eyes and walk in the dark."
As I turn to the shadows in my own life,
I cease reacting and resisting,

When I resisted the darkness, the shadows,
seeking light somewhere else,
I remained separate from what is,
from God.

My shadows,
which I previously counted as adversaries,
became
my most profound teachers.

Silence

I've had it all wrong.

Creation and the sounds of creation
have not replaced Silence;
They are bathed in Silence;
They are awash in Silence.

Silence is audible to me and all,
at all times, in all places.

Silence is
When I hear inwardly;
Sounds are what I hear outwardly.

Silence is the framework, the background
of Creation.
Sounds are the servants and purveyors
of Mistress Silence.

Sounds confirm for me
that Silence is,
that Silence is rare,
that Silence is vital to my Quest.

Sounds are but bubbles

on her (Silence) surface,
which burst,
but give evidence to the strong undercurrent.

Sounds are but a faint utterance of Silence
agreeable only when
they contrast with her and relieve her.

Sounds can be intensifiers of Silence
When Harmonious and Melodic.

Silence is my refuge,
A sequel to dull talk and foolish acts.
Silence is a salve for my every sorrow.
I welcome her
after joy as well as disappointment.

Silence is the background,
which I as life painter may not alter.
However awkward the picture I paint in the foreground of life,
Silence remains true and inviolable
as my background.

In attempting to help others,
when I can put aside my individuality,
I am most eloquent
when I am most silent.

When I listen
while I speak,
I become a hearer
along with the others

and

healing takes place.

Someone

Someone to blaze the trail for you,
Someone to pick you up and
carry you on your way,
Someone strong, in control,
and fully confident,
Someone who is a leader
you can follow,
Someone to remove your pain and sorrow,

I am not.

Someone to walk with you,
to accompany you on your journey,
Someone to help
who will help you,
Someone as lost and
as thirsty as you,
Someone to trust,
Someone who loves you,
whom you can love,

Am I.

Choose me?

Spark

Holy Spirit

as wind

from where?

to where?

Will fan
the

Spark
of

True Love

into a raging inferno

and

blow out
the

flickering fire focused on self.

Wind on the Water

Watching the water
ripple, swirl, and bounce about
in the wind,

I ask,

Is what I see
the wind?
the water's reaction to the wind?
or
the wind and the water becoming one?

If the wind is like the Holy Spirit
and I am the water,

Are my actions in the Spirit

the actions of the Holy Spirit?
my reaction to the Holy Spirit?
or
the Holy Spirit and I becoming One?

Stand and Stare

So often, I failed to see
what was right in front of me.
So often, I overlooked
the beauty of a flower,
the marvel of an insect,
the ever changing cloud patterns in the sky,
the splendor of a bird,
the majesty of a pine,
the deep blues and greens of the lake.

I seemed to busy to notice,
rushing dashing, planning,
being busy with
no time to
stand and stare.

Jesus knew how to stand and stare.

He relished the beauty of the lilies
and the birds of the air.
He marvelled
how a tiny mustard seed grows into a tree.
He knew how moth and woodworm destroy,
how yeast leavens bread,
how a weed chokes.

He noticed
how farmers scatter seed,
how a woman searches for a lost coin,
Zaccheus in the sycamore,
all the children,
and beggars and lepers.

Because He took time to
stand and stare,
Jesus could sense the presence of God.
the work of the Creator.

To be alive to the world
is to be alive to
the One who makes all things
and
fills them with His presence,

if I simply
Stand and Stare.

Story

All moments are key.

Life itself is grounded in the mystery of God
and full of Divine Grace.

Each person's story
is scripture
waiting to be read and interpreted.

Each person's story
is sacred text
revealing Divine Truth.

What is needed is
Eyes that see,
Ears that hear.

Once we have made peace with them,
Even the saddest things
can be a source of Wisdom and Strength.

To lose touch
with one's own story
is to risk
losing touch

with God.
To keep that story in mind
is to remain open to
the sacred book
God is co-writing with each of us,
the book of our lives.

Stray

To whom do I belong?
To God?
To the world?

I said God, but
the voices of the world were loud,
full of promises,
very seductive.

I needed to go out into the world and
prove something.
I needed to prove that I was worth loving
by being successful,
powerful,
popular.

The world told me
I had to earn love
through hard work and determination.
The voices pushed me
to gain acceptance and love
by being busy,
productive,
successful.

The voices denied my inherent belovedness
and pulled me off my path.

Then,
Helping others,
I began to heal,
to get back on my path.
I knew I was forgiven for straying.

Loving others,
I began to remember I was loved,
that I was beloved.
I began to feel peace,
peace beyond any understanding.
I felt grace.

God chose to heal me
even though I was so out of touch
spiritually.

Now,
what seemed so important was not:
Success,
What people said about me,
How I looked,
How much money or possessions I had,
All the outward worldly signs.

Those things stripped away,
I am a tiny little battered soul,
Alive and kept alive by
the Breath of the Holy Spirit.
My soul is what matters;
It is priceless.

Love, Hope, Confidence, Joy
flow now.
Like Lazarus,
I am alive again.
Like the Prodigal Son,
I am no longer lost.
I rejoice.
God rejoices.

The Stream

I sat and watched the flowing water,
listening to its rush.
Seems like I've seen it or heard it
a long time.

Although I'd had plenty to eat and drink,
I was thirsty.
The water seemed so inviting,
fresh, cool, clear.

As much as I'd had to eat and drink,
my thirst was not quenched.
I'd explored up and down the stream,
but I never found its source
or knew where it ended,
if it did.

Funny thing about the stream is that
despite being so close,
it's too far down to scoop up a handful of water.
And the steep bank
does not allow me to just get my feet wet.

Only way to taste or experience the stream,
it seems,

is to just jump in.
Trouble is,
the stream is fast flowing;
I don't know how deep it is;
and I don't know where it leads,
where the current will take me.

I'm tired of being a bystander.
I'll have to leave every thing behind.
But I'll see new sights,
ride the rapids,
and maybe quench my thirst,
maybe.
But I'll have to leave my things behind;
skinny-dippers only allowed in.

Can't pull anyone in with me either;
they might drown.
They've got to decide on their own.
Would be tough holding on to each other
traveling downstream anyway.

I'm going in!
Splash.

Wow, it's deep;
Can't touch bottom.

And is it ever moving fast.

Lots of bystanders
along shore.

Some are concerned
and even try to throw me

a lifesaver.
Come on in!
Water's fine!
They don't seem to believe me.

Stream quickly takes me out of range
onward.

Water tastes great,
but still does not quench my thirst;
maybe downstream,
wherever that is.

This is true freedom,
not attached at all.

Don't know where I'm headed,
but somehow it does not seem important.
I'm enjoying the flow,
seeing the sights,
feeling ecstatic.

Left everything behind,
but really didn't need them
for this trip.

Come on in!
Water's fine!

Where am I headed?
I don't know.

But,
now at least,
I'm in the flow.

The Sun

Is it not curious that

I cannot look directly at that

by whose light

I can see everything.

Who's terms?

Take Joy
in what Life has to offer
on *its* terms.

We make the journey
constantly trying to
mold life into our own terms.
In doing so,
We are frustrated
as the Cosmos does not bend to our will
and/or
We completely miss out on
The Joy life has to offer us.

Accept
Whatever Life has to offer
on *its* terms
and
EnJoy Life!

Thirst

Every new lead,
Each new connection,
Every new contact
leads
Not to answers,
Not to certainty,
But only
More Questions.

The apparent quenching of a momentary thirst
is only the creation
of a new, even greater, thirst.

Although not raising new questions
by not following new leads or
making new contacts
is an option,
It is only a trap.

A quenched thirst
only leads to dehydration
of the soul.

Desiring to be sated
in this life

is to miss the mark.
The journey

is one of thirst;
Me for Love (God)
and
God for me.

Together

Try and put me in your box
and you'll kill me;
there are no horizons
within it.

Stay safe and secure
within it
or
come fly with me
among the stars.

My Friend, the Tree

My friend the Tree
teaches me much of life.

It stands tall, proud of what it is,
not wanting to be anything other than
what God made it to be.

It remains true to itself
in all weather, good and bad,
warm and cold,
calm and stormy,
dry and wet.
It bends in the winds to survive,
but remains true to its roots and
grows towards its creator.

It thrives in all seasons,
blossoming in spring,
growing anew in summer,
glowing in the fall, and
dancing with winter's winds.

It is happy as tree
providing shelter for some,
food for others,

visual delight for many,
shade for the weary, and
joy for all.

My friend the Tree.
Would that I could emulate it.
It teaches so many lessons
without uttering a word,
just by the way it lives.

My friend, the Tree.

Trust

When I trust God
to act in me,
God acts in me.

This must be
how our lives become prophetic.

When I am open to the Holy Spirit,
The Spirit leads me
where God wants me to go.

Unquenchable?

My thirst consumes me.

And the more I drink,
the more I thirst.

Prayer begets prayer;
Spiritual connections, the need to connect more;
Readings lead to other readings;
Helping those in grief, the call to help more.
Sharing allows others to share
calling me to share even more.

Relax, meditate?
I do, but
it inflames my thirst,
increases my zeal,
excites me more
drives me on and on
to
Help, pray, read, share, act
with compassion and zeal.

I'm asked,
"For what are you searching?"

All I know is
what it is *not*.

It is not
accomplishment, acquisition, attainment, arrival.

Each new taste of God (Love)
increases my yearning,
expands my desire,
magnifies my zeal,
explodes my craving,
consumes me.

God must be thirsting for me.

Value

A quarter fell out of my pants pocket the other night.
I looked at it on the floor and
remembered how
it would get me into the movies,
provide popcorn and a pop
and leave me change.

T'was a Long time ago,
but the quarter itself has not changed.
(Oh it has in appearance, but it still represents
twenty-five pennies and a fourth of a dollar.)

But the value we place on it
—its meaning to us–
has changed dramatically.
(Won't even pay for a phone call now.)

Are life's events like that?
Might we assign great value to an event
or precious little?
The experience is the experience
is the experience.
The key question is
its worth to me.

A quarter was a quarter is a quarter.
A rainstorm can be
a Broadway extravaganza
or
a nap.

Viking Way

Sky ablaze
with a fiery red/orange sunset.
Warm mild breezes
filling the sails.
Sounds of water
up against the sailboat.
Gulls
looking for a handout.

Flaming arrows stalking
the target pyre.

Sails afire!

Boat crackling with fire.

A burial with honor.

Boat and body sink;
flames go water black
as the sun sinks
below the far horizon.

A day and a man
are gone.

Both were enjoyed;

None to follow
will be the same.

Whirlpool

To jump into the whirlpool; to let go of all my handholds, all
the
things I've collected to make me feel secure; to have complete
faith and trust in my Creator knowing that God's Love for
me will see me through these trials that I now face;
to accept the fact that I don't know where I'm
going or how I'm going to get there; to
jump in over my head; to accept the
rough journey, the dizziness, the
uncertainty; to ride God's
flow; to go deeper and
deeper within; to
let go of all my
attachments;
to find my
God deep
within
me.

Who?

Dear God,
Who am I?
Who am I really?

Dear John,
Despite the good–and sometimes bad–things you do,
You are not what you do.
Despite the good–and sometimes bad–things people say about
you,
You are not what people say you are.

John,
You are one–in Love–with me
deep within
(as is everyone else.)

Love,
God

Wholeness

Devil comes from the Greek Diabolos.

Diabolos means to throw apart.

Is evil, separation?

When I separate myself from others;
that is evil.

When I keep my material life separate from
my spirituality;
that is evil.

When I address the needs of my body apart from
my soul;
that is evil.

Holiness comes from Wholeness.

Wholeness is integrity.

When I help, share with,
and join others;
that is wholeness.

When all my actions are governed by
my spirituality;
that is holiness.

When Soul heals body;
that is wholeness.

Separation is evil;
Wholeness is
Integrity is
Unity is
Holiness.

Winds

When sailing troubled waters,
I am tempted to find safe ports of call.
But I must trust,
stay the course,
let my sails stand tall.

I must use the guidance given,
sail by the stars,
follow God's chart,
for the joy is not in arriving,
but in following my heart.

The schooner that is me
is best not ashore,
but riding strong winds
and asking for more.

Prayer

In prayer,
I discovered what I already had.

I pray where I am,
deepen what I have and
realize I am already there.

I have everything I need
and
I never knew it.

Wonder

For me,

The awesomeness of the Creator,
The joyfulness of the Savior,
The wonder of the Holy Spirit

is that

I, in my brokeness,
I, in my finitude,
I, in my weaknesses and with my many imperfections,

can be made an

Instrument of God's Love
and
Healing Power
for
The Bereaved.

It is breathtaking
and
Truly Wonder-full.

Thanks, God!

Communicate

How do I express this?
How do I explain what's happened,
what's happening.
Some of these feelings, these experiences
are totally new.
If not new,
then with new intensity.
Words
are inadequate.
Words seem
incompetent
to describe this.

So why try?
I must try,
but I'll give up on words.
You can see it
in my eyes,
hear it,
in my voice,
feel it
in my touch,
taste it,
in my tears,
sense it,

in my being.

What has happened,
what is happening
defines me,
is defining me–
indescribably.

To get any idea of what
has happened,
is happening to me,
Be one with me.

I know no other way.

Poem

A poem

exists with me,
dying to get out,
to be born.

I ache to give it birth,
life.

Every one I have written so far
seems but a preview,
a hint
of the one that is me.

Can I write it?
Can it be written?

Is that poem me?
My life?

Can I simply live it?

No, no!
I must some how write it,
bring it to life.

I must end this ache,
live this life,
write this poem.

Having lived my life fully,
will my poem thus
be written?